Also by Jess Keating

**How to Outrun a Crocodile
When Your Shoes Are Untied**

**How to Outswim a Shark
Without a Snorkel**

Praise for *How to Outrun a Crocodile When Your Shoes Are Untied*

2015 Red Maple Award Nominee

2015–2016 Georgia Children's Book Award Finalist

"As if junior high isn't enough of a zoo, Jess Keating's debut...[is] a menagerie of laugh-out-loud antics and relatable tween woes."

—Anna Staniszewski, author of *The Dirt Diary*

"A wild romp, filled with humor and heart."

—Lisa Schroeder, author of *It's Raining Cupcakes* and the Charmed Life series

"Debut author Keating delivers a fun-filled, pitch-perfect book... Humor, poignancy, and fascinating zoological facts infuse the narrative with a warm, conversational tone... An amusing, highly readable book about the perils of being twelve in a snake-eat-snake world."

—*Kirkus*, Starred Review

"An absolutely perfect summer read."

—*Girls' Life Magazine.com*

"Deals with the hardships of junior high in a funny and zany, yet thoughtful, manner. True animal facts that are interspersed throughout the story add wit and provide the reader with some new information. This novel is a must-have...highly recommended."

—*Library Media Connection*

Praise for *How to Outswim a Shark Without a Snorkel*

"Keating perfectly captures the fears, awkwardness, and excitement of being twelve and delivers a positive story with plenty of humor that emphasizes thinking for and becoming comfortable with oneself."

—*Booklist*

"Keating maintains the same humorous, lightly soul-searching tone, perfect for a barely teenage girl."

—*Kirkus Reviews*

"Daydream about summer this winter with Jess Keating's latest read... Ana Wright is back and better than ever in the second book to the My Life Is a Zoo series."

—*Girls' Life Magazine.com*

HOW TO
OUTFOX
YOUR
FRIENDS
WHEN YOU
DON'T HAVE A
CLUE

Jess Keating

sourcebooks
jabberwocky

Published by Sourcebooks Jabberwocky an imprint of Sourcebooks, Inc.
P.O. Box 4410, Naperville, Illinois 60567–4410
(630) 961–3900
Fax: (630) 961–2168
www.jabberwockykids.com

Library of Congress Cataloging-in-Publication data is on file with the publisher.

Source of Production: Versa Press, East Peoria, Illinois, USA
Date of Production: August 2015
Run Number: 5004660

Printed and bound in the United States of America.

VP 10 9 8 7 6 5 4 3 2 1

To you, dear reader, and your friends, both old and new.

"A man's friendships are one of the best measures of his worth."

—*Charles Darwin*

Okay, Charlie. Even though I agree with you here, can I just ask why practically *every* old-timey quote we have to read in our textbooks is always written about "a MAN'S" this or "a MAN'S" that? Yes, friends are important, blah, blah, blah. But come on, if you're going to make some big statement, couldn't you include—oh, I don't know—*half* of the world in it? Where are all the deep quotes about girls? Or can't you just say "a *person's* friendships"? I know you probably don't mean anything by it, and I think you're cool and all. But this is the twenty-first century, and you're supposed to be one of the greatest minds of all time. I mean, I wouldn't have named my parrot after you if I didn't think you had some good ideas. But I expect more from you. Mainly because you don't fly around and poop on my head like MY Darwin.

Chapter 1

Red foxes communicate with each other by making "scent posts," by peeing on trees or rocks to announce their presence.

—Animal Wisdom

Oh, gross! Imagine if humans communicated with each other like that. Everywhere you went you'd have to pee on everything. I'd much rather announce my presence with an awesome sound track like when celebrities walk onstage during talk shows. In fact, I wish I had a cool sound track that followed me everywhere, so I sounded supercool every time I entered a room. That beats peeing, right?

Know what's crazy?

In exactly nine days, four hours, and nineteen minutes, I am going to *change*.

And I don't mean like a tiny, silly change, like getting a haircut, or finding a pair of pants that makes your butt look awesome (although I wouldn't turn that down), or even finding out that you aced a math exam for the first time in your life, so you can actually impress your supercute genius boyfriend with your whip-smart intelligence for once.

No. I mean a *big* change.

Teenager big.

That's right.

This is the last week of my *life* that I will be a non-teenager. I mean, at least until I turn twenty, but that's a million years away still, so it doesn't count. But next week? I'm the big one three.

Say it with me: thir-*teen*.

The *teen* is right there in the word.

Not to brag, but I think I'm handling it pretty well. I haven't had any meltdowns about getting old yet, and I was only mildly wigged out when I caught Mom looking at photo albums of Daz and I as babies with shiny tears in her eyes. I mean, it's not like I'm *dying* or anything, right?

Just turning thirteen.

Even though I'll never be "preteen" again for the rest of my life.

And I'll never be able to order stuff on the kids' menu at Spaghetti Joe's again, because they are seriously strict about that age cutoff nonsense on the menu, and I *love* the mini-meatballs they make especially for the kid's plate.

And being thirteen will mean I'm officially too old to get into movies at the supercheap price, which is a real shame considering it costs more than my allowance for even *one* stupid ticket. That's not even counting the popcorn.

What good is a movie without popcorn?

Ugh.

Maybe I should think about the *positive* side of thirteen. Like how in all the movies, it's when the kid turns thirteen that they find out they have superpowers or are demigods and all that. Maybe I'm a week away from finding out Dad is actually a Greek god. Being thirteen might not be so bad if I can control lightning bolts, right?

Of course, most almost-thirteen-year-olds don't also have to instruct their friends on how to avoid getting drooled on by a giraffe, but hey, welcome to my life.

"Hold your hand flat," I said, shoving Ashley's arm farther over the chain-link fence. She was gripping the clump of alfalfa hay so tightly, her knuckles were white. Both of my parents work at the zoo, so as long as I ask the keepers, I'm usually allowed to hang out with the animals if my homework is done.

"She's going to bite off my hand, I know it," Ashley said, edging closer to me. "Do they eat meat too?"

The funny thing about being friends with your former nemesis is that every so often, you can get a real kick out of scaring them with totally non-scary things.

Like innocent giraffes.

"Only when they're extra hungry," I said, keeping my voice low and serious. "And you have to watch out for their fangs," I added. "They're retractable, and if they bite you, you could be dead within thirty seconds. It's a special mammal venom."

"*What?!*" Ashley yelped. She stumbled back, dropping the handful of hay to the ground as she tripped over my toes. "Are you freakin' kidding me?! You've got me sticking my hand out to some monster with *fangs*, what's wrong with—"

I smirked.

The way Ashley's eyebrows squished together like little angry caterpillars always made me giggle.

The realization that I was messing with her dawned on her face as I picked up the hay and handed it to Paisley, who happily responded by licking my hand clean with her dark-blue tongue. I bit my lip to keep from laughing, but that didn't stop the snort from escaping. Times like this, I wish I could plaster a fake halo above my head to play up the innocent part.

"You're the *worst*," she huffed, brushing off her knees. She glared at me, but unlike six months ago, it wasn't a *real* glare, where she wanted me to drop dead. It was more of a playful glare. At least it was playful compared to what I know Ashley's glares are capable of. Back in seventh grade, a patented Ashley glare was enough to make me lose two years of my life span.

Three Things I Didn't Know about My Former Nemesis until I Accidentally-on-Purpose Jumped into a Shark Tank over the Summer to Save Her from Embarrassment

1. Even though Ashley used to seriously hate me (and yeah, I admit, I didn't like her either and almost embarrassed her in front of a massive crowd of people at the zoo), we actually aren't *that* different. We both agree on the importance of a good lip gloss (although I prefer the ones that aren't all shiny and she *loves* those ones). And we also both love hammerhead sharks. Lip

gloss and hammerhead sharks might seem like a weird combo, but maybe that right there is why we ended up friends after all.

2. Ashley is *crazy* good at picking out clothes and doing her hair, and it's not because she naturally looks great all the time like some sort of perma-photoshopped model. She actually spends time doing it, the way some people study math or learn how to garden. Don't get the wrong idea though—I'm a total fashion *don't* myself, which is why it's pretty cool to have someone in my life who knows the difference between boot cut and straight cut. And no, I don't remember it, so don't ask me.

3. A few months ago when school started, I was worried that despite being friends in the summer, she was going to morph back into a Sneerer and throw chicken parm at me like old times. But you know what? She didn't. I have this theory that the minute someone jumps into a shark tank to save you from embarrassment, you're bonded for life. Ashley must agree too, because even though she's had lots of chances to make fun of me in school, instead she just blinks at me and shakes her head when I do something goofbally, like try to do the robot dance in the hallway. Sometimes you need to dance.

"You know, you should be thankful I'm even interested in feeding some smelly giraffe," she huffed. "I don't see anyone *else* here with you, do you? Like you don't get enough of the weird animals at home now."

"Yeah, yeah," I said, wiping the giraffe drool onto my jeans. She wasn't exactly wrong. Ever since we'd moved out of the zoo when summer ended, it was sort of weird not to wake up to the sound of grumpy lions in the morning. Too bad I couldn't trade my weirdo twin brother, Daz, for them. I handed her a chunk of sweet potato. "Here, try this. She likes it more than the hay."

Ashley held her palm flat like I had showed her, sucking in a breath when Paisley nuzzled her snout along her fingertips to grab it.

"There you go," she cooed to the giraffe. "See, you're much nicer than mean old Ana says. I bet she's just miffed Kevin hasn't kissed her yet, isn't she?" She glanced at me haughtily and cocked an eyebrow.

"For the hundredth time," I said, "I am *not* upset about not kissing Kevin yet! I told you, I'm *done* trying to make that happen. And we have a perfectly good time *not* kissing, *thankyouverymuch*."

Honestly, despite what you might have heard about almost-thirteen-year-old girls, we aren't *obsessed* about boys the way all those girlie magazines seem to think we are. I mean, yeah. I think Kevin is awesome, and he still gives me that swirly-vertigo feeling when he stares at me with his dark eyes after his mom drops us off from our group date, but *seriously*, how much good night kissing can you expect to do with your idiot brother whooping from the bushes telling you to "get a room"? It was bad enough when we lived in the zoo next to the hippos, but it turns out that living back in our old house is just as embarrassing.

"Are you not even a *little* interested to see what it's like? You've been together for months! I mean, we're pretty much women now," Ashley said, searching for a carrot and carefully holding it out for Paisley.

The way she said "women" made my stomach turn. It's funny. I could see myself as a little kid because I have pictures of what I used to look like. (Yes, the pigtails and goofball glasses were totally embarrassing. Thank the lemurs for contact lenses.)

But when it came to picturing myself as a grown-up? That's a whole other story. I had no pictures to look at; how could I possibly know *how* I should be as a "woman"? Would I look like Mom? Would I know how to walk in high heels like those ladies on the red carpet in Hollywood? Are we supposed to know how to magically become teenagers too? Am I going to wake up one morning and *know* that it's the right time to kiss Kevin for the first time? Will I know how to put on dark eyeliner without jabbing myself in the eye so Mom doesn't think I woke up with pinkeye too?

The whole thing was exhausting.

I shook my head, confused by the image of me as a grown-up. "I told you. I've learned my lesson." I put the plastic lid on Paisley's food container and clicked it shut. "The last time I tried to grow up at warp speed and kiss him, I head-butted him."

Ashley's lips squished together. "I know I promised you I would never laugh at that, but..." Her mouth quivered.

"And then"—I lifted my eyebrows, drawing out the moment—"he got a *nosebleed*." I grinned with pride as Ashley cackled at my expense. It may not be the greatest first almost-kiss story, but now that a few months had passed, I could definitely see the humor.

Sort of.

Especially because Kevin didn't move out of state to get away from me after that whole thing.

Anyway.

"It's nice not having to worry about that stuff," I admitted. "It will happen when it happens, you know?" I said proudly.

Ashley gave me her usual "Are you freaking

kidding me?" look, but the truth was, I felt pretty darn mature saying that. It's something Mom says all the time, and it used to annoy the you-know-what out of me. But now, I think I get it. I liked getting to hang out with Kev and hold hands when we go to the movies together (even though Daz always hogs the Sour Patch Kids). So for me, the whole first kiss thing could wait.

Maybe that means I'm ready to be a teenager after all?

As Ashley and I made our way to the back of the giraffe enclosure, my phone buzzed.

I dug into my jacket pocket, enjoying the brief feeling of warmth on my fingertips. It was probably Mom telling me we were having her famous Tuna Surprise for dinner (the surprise is, it *sucks*), but a different name had popped up on the screen.

Reading the message, I sighed in annoyance.

DAZMANIAN DEVIL: Hey, loser! Have you seen my new scorpion? He's out of his cage again. Get back here and help me look. PS Mom says you're in charge of setting up for dinner, hahaha.

I shook my head, tucking my phone back in my pocket. "*Ugh*," I said. That pretty much summed it all up when it came to Daz.

"What's up?" Ashley asked. "Is it Kevin? Is he dumping you because you haven't kissed him yet?" She swung her leg over her bike, looking downright pleased at herself for that little joke.

"It's Daz," I said. "This is the third time in a week his scorpion has escaped from his cage. And *every* time, it winds up in my laundry pile."

She blinked at me, clearly confused.

"I don't even know." I threw up my hands.

Sometimes people think that because we don't live in the zoo anymore, our house wasn't jam-packed with all sorts of animals. But really, we still *had* a zoo, including two tarantulas, a pet boa constrictor named Oscar, four toads, seven other snakes, and Daz's latest addition, a scorpion named Dwayne "The Rock" Johnson.

Seriously, he makes us call him by his whole name.

Ashley gave me a sympathetic look as I zipped my coat tighter to protect against the cold November air. "Dude. Do you ever just look at your family and think that you're adopted?" She wrapped her scarf around her chin.

I swiped a stray piece of goobery giraffe hay from my mittens. "*All* the time."

Chapter 2

A lynx's toes spread when they step on the snow, acting like natural snowshoes.

—Animal Wisdom

I can pick up pencils with my toes. Does that count?

Hamlet is:
A) a prince
B) a princess
C) a king
D) a potato

You know, as someone who has sat on crocodiles, jumped into shark tanks, and routinely finds six-foot snakes in her bed, it takes surprisingly little to freak me out. The word *bikini*, that slimy gunk stuck in the drain after you do dishes, and Daz's dirty shoes all over the front hallway are enough to make me break into a cold sweat. But today's panic attack is brought to you by one man: William Shakespeare.

I know. He's *dead*, and yet he's still able to stress me out from the grave. I get that he's supposed to be super famous and has all these fancy-schmancy plays and sonnets and all that (what the heck is a sonnet?!), but *seriously*, could he maybe chill with the "thou art" this, and the "twixt" that? What kind of a writer uses the word *usurp'st*? Or names someone *Polonius*?!

Doesn't that sound like some sort of disease carried by mosquitoes or what?

Please.

We'd been covering Shakespeare for a week, and I have to admit it was making me feel pretty stupid. I have no idea how people make sense of this stuff.

I thought eighth grade was supposed to be all cool parties, bigger lockers, and getting to feel like a superstar because we were *finally* at the top of the junior high food chain. Nobody mentioned ol' Bill and his bag of jumbly word tricks would be marching in to ruin my day with a test. It was the last day of our Shakespeare unit, and Mr. Nicholson *loves* his tests. Of course, it's also the one test I completely forgot to study for.

I tapped my pen on my paper and started to circle an answer. Hamlet was definitely a king. No, wait. A prince.

King.

Prince.

My hand wavered back and forth over the answers as I darted a look at Ashley. She was sitting across from me, and I could tell by the way her eyebrows weren't scrunched up that she wasn't having any problems with the quiz. In fact, it looked like she was now happily doodling on the margins of the page. A few seats down, Bella was fiddling with the tips of her short hair while her other hand moved swiftly down the page marking off answers. Was I the only person in this entire room who didn't get this Hamlet guy?

Hrmph.

"Eyes on your own paper, please." Mr. Nicholson's low warning jolted me back to my test. Did he say that because of *me*? I wasn't cheating—I was only *glancing*, but not at papers! I wanted to peek up at my teacher's face, so he could see I wasn't at all guilty, but the scorching-hot pain in my ears probably meant I looked as guilty as a wolf on a sheep farm anyway.

CREATURE FILE

SPECIES NAME: *Nicholsonian Academicus*

KINGDOM: The classroom. (One time I saw him at the grocery store buying kiwis, but I'm not including that because it was sort of awkward seeing him out of his usual classroom habitat. Also, kiwis are weird and their skin makes my mouth itch.)

PHYLUM: Teachers who are giant nerd-balls, but it's okay because deep down you really love those funny little stickers that they put on tests when you do well.

WEIGHT: Including or not including the sweater-vest-tie combo?

FEEDS ON: Pop quizzes; those little balls of cheese wrapped in red wax; smiles from Ms. Fenton (pretty sure he has a crush on her).

LIFE SPAN: Based on the kiwi and cheese diet, he's probably pretty healthy.

HANDLING TECHNIQUE: *Nicholsonian Academicus* is even-tempered and nice. Loves it when you participate in class (even if your answer is wrong); strictly against gum chewing.

I circled an answer without thinking and peeked at my watch. I have no idea how watches work, but you can bet there's a snail inside mine, turning a crank and making the seconds tick by as mind-numbingly slow as possible. You know, Kevin is always going on about this guy Stephen Hawking, who has all these theories on space and time and all that. I bet that he could tell me why time slows down during boring school stuff and speeds up when you're actually having fun.

"Time's up!" Mr. Nicholson announced, clapping his hands together once.

I clutched my pen tighter as he walked up the aisles to sweep the tests from our desks and into a pile on his green folder.

When the tests were in a ncat pile on the quiz shelf, Mr. Nicholson leaned against his desk. His eyes were dancing with excitement, which meant one thing and one thing only: he had a new project for us.

"Okay, guys. I know since you're such excellent, intelligent students, you're probably wondering what your major project will be this month," he said, rolling his eyes playfully, pretending like he was appeasing us by spilling the beans.

I giggled, while the boys in the class booed. You had to hand it to Mr. Nicholson—he sure liked his own jokes.

"I've given a lot of thought to your November projects, and I think I've got just the thing for a group of students who are sick of Mr. Shakespeare." He eyed the room expectantly. "Am I right?!"

"*Yesss!*" we all chimed, with my own voice ringing loudest.

Anything but Shakespeare, pleeeease.

"Good!" He clasped his hands together. "So we're going to switch gears here. Since this is your last year of junior high before heading off to high school, I thought it would be nice if you did a little *reflection*."

Cue the moaning.

"Now hold on a minute," he said. He scrawled the word *influence* on the board in large, swoopy letters.

"For one Superman eraser"—he held up the tiny eraser from the jar he kept on his desk—"who can tell me what *influence* means?"

Brooke's hand popped up. "Influence is the stuff that has an effect on you. Like, that changes you." She caught my eye as she spoke, smiling.

"Bingo!" he said, tossing her the eraser. "Have any of you ever thought back about your early childhood? What you were like at five years old? Or even ten years old? Who can share what influenced you at that age?"

Imaginary crickets filled my head as Mr. Nicholson scanned the room. My palms itched with sweat. I knew as well as everyone else did that if nobody volunteered to answer, we would be volun*told* to speak up. Personally, my early childhood was filled with reptiles peeing on my head and Daz trapping me in the washing machine, so yeah. Delicate cycle, my butt.

I kept my eyes down.

Bella lifted her hand hesitantly. I grinned into my notes; I knew Bella was trying to be braver in class, so it made my heart happy to see her answering more questions. Mr. Nicholson noticed too, snapping his fingers and pointing. "Bella! You're up!"

She blinked at her desk but spoke clearly. "Um, I loved Egyptian stuff as a little kid," she said tentatively. "I guess you could say that influenced me. I tried to cut my hair like Cleopatra once."

Mr. Nicholson tossed her a tiny snail eraser. "Yes! That's a great example." I caught Bella's eye and gave her a sneaky thumbs-up beside my desk.

He scanned the room again, observing our blank faces. "You know, Cleopatra was the last pharaoh of Ancient Egypt, renowned for her beauty. Sort of like a Kardashian, only this was long before the time of all your iPods and iPads and iThingies. Write this down." He cleared his throat dramatically. "Cleopatra did *not* take selfies."

The class tittered. Mr. Nicholson could be pretty cool for an old guy.

"When I was a little kid, I was influenced by Batman," he said, gathering a stack of papers from his desk. "I wanted to wear a cape everywhere and tried to go around fighting crime. In fact…" he said, leaning over to lift the bottom of his pant leg. "Some things never change."

The class gasped in goofy delight as he showed off the bright-yellow bat signal on his socks.

"Nice!" Eric exclaimed, nodding with approval. I couldn't help but agree. For some reason, knowing my teacher was a giant nerd made me feel a lot more comfortable with my own inner geek-ball.

He grinned. "You see? Sometimes the things that influence us stick with us for life. Sometimes they're temporary and help us get through certain stages. Each of us is different, and *because* you guys are almost halfway through the year and going into big, bad high school next year, I thought now was the perfect opportunity to mark your time in eighth grade by creating something to show me who, or what, influences you now. It will be like a time capsule of sorts that you can look back on when you're old and gray."

He began handing out the papers to the front of every row, making sure every student got one. I swiped the crisp paper from my desk and carefully stuck it in my binder, handing the rest of the pile behind me. Mr. Nicholson's usual bold, dark font stared back at me, outlining the project along with some fill-in-the-blank prompts to help us begin.

Five Influences in My Life— A Media Project by:

Already my mind was buzzing with ideas. As much work as new projects were, there was something deliciously *fun* about starting something different. Like having a gigantic sandwich in front of you that you couldn't *wait* to dig into.

Ashley's hand shot up. "Um, Mr. Nicholson?" I could tell by the way her cheek puffed out a little that she was doing her best to hide her gum. Mr. Nicholson *hated* gum.

"Yes, Ashley?" He looked up from his own handout.

"What exactly does the 'media' part mean?" she asked, holding up the sheet. "It says here, 'A Media Project'?" Ashley squinted suspiciously.

"Good question," he said, sitting on his desk. "Does anyone know what media is?"

I lifted my hand. "Is it a way of communicating?" I ventured.

He tossed me a tiny unicorn eraser. "You got it. Media is the plural for medium. But not like 'in the middle' medium like an order of fries. This is stuff like newspapers, blog posts, videos, newscasts, magazines. Those are all forms of media. Once you've decided on your influences—and they can be people, places, things, even fictional characters—I want you to use one of the types of media listed to tell me about them."

A small grin curled at my lips. As far as projects went, this one rated pretty high on the Awesome Scale.

Mr. Nicholson continued. "As you can see from your handout, you'll have two weeks to hand in your project, and it can be *any* of the forms listed here. And…drumroll please!" He started to drum his fingers on the desk beneath him. "You will present your projects, and they will be displayed in the foyer at the end of the month!"

Well, if the media thing didn't get a bunch of moans out of us, *that* sure did. Immediately, hands shot in the air. I sat back, watching in amusement as the chaos unfolded.

A few months ago, the thought of everyone seeing my project would have made me lose my lunch. Go figure that performing in front of an audience all summer with sharks swarming you gets rid of that fear pretty darn quick. School projects were nothing compared to waddling around in a scuba suit with strangers gawking at you.

Mr. Nicholson shushed us. "To answer your

question, *yes*, all projects will be displayed, and *yes*, you will have to say a few words about it for credit. This part *is* mandatory, but it's only a short chat. It's not a presidential address." He gave us a sneaky smile. "I'm not *that* mean. And, for the first time ever, I'm introducing a 'Get out of Jail Free' card for the presentations."

Everyone exchanged confused looks. "What does that mean?" someone asked from the back. "Do we get to not do the project?"

"Nice try!" He laughed. "But there will be three faculty from three classes there to listen to all of your presentations. The student who receives the highest marks from all of us will get to have their lowest test score dropped for your final grades at the end of the semester."

Ashley's eyes lit up. "For real? You won't count a bad grade? On *any* test?"

Mr. Nicholson nodded. "Any of our biweekly tests, that's right. I know some of you could use the boost, so this is a chance to make up for it. Each project will be submitted with a written piece about *why* you chose that medium and what you're expressing through it. What I'll need from you by Wednesday is a two-paragraph proposal on your choice of media and your list of influences, okay?" he said. "I've also included a suggested time line so you can use it to check off every step. Because I'm nice like that. Any questions?" He stood up again and leaned back casually in the way that always makes him look like a jeans model.

Zack's hand shot in the air. "Can we talk about *anything* anything?"

I rolled my eyes. I swear, I wish I could use one of those little unicorn erasers of Mr. Nicholson's to erase some of my past, because my crush on Zack should never have happened. He's a total jerk. Funny how a guy whose name you had scrawled all over your binder can turn out to be a waste of ink. It was clear from the way his handout was already half-crumpled on his desk that he hadn't bothered to read it yet. He was leaning back on his chair so only two legs were on the ground, with his trademark bright-orange hoodie zipped tight to his chin. *Loser.*

"Four legs on the ground, Zack." Mr. Nicholson walked over and reached for his paper, smoothing it out as he spoke. "Anything within reason, yes. I'd like you to use this as a way to explore newspapers or film or even the Internet, as a way to teach us about what influences you. Which is precisely what is says right here." He tapped the page. Zack's ears turned pink. "The possibilities are endless!"

Settling back in my chair, I began to conjure up

what the perfect project might look like. What were five things that influenced me? And what kind of media should I use?

I turned in my chair, eyeing Bella. She was hunched over, already scribbling wildly in her notebook. A few chairs over, Ashley was tapping her desk while inspecting her cuticles. When she noticed me looking, she stuck out her tongue in a goofy face.

I held back my laugh. Bella and Ashley were both so different, but I couldn't imagine the past few months without them.

That's when it hit me. Some ideas bubble up inside you in a slow, fizzy rush. But sometimes they hit you like a stampeding buffalo. This was one of those buffalo ideas.

I could do my project on my friends! Bella, Ashley, Liv—they all influence me so much!

It was perfect. Not only would it be super easy (because, *hello*, they're my friends, and I wouldn't need to Wikipedia anything!), but it would also be great to talk about them more. My life had changed so much since summer, and Bella and Ashley were sort of like surprises the world gave me, especially when Liv moved away. Okay, that sounds totally cheesy, but if it weren't for them, I'd probably still be holed up in a corner somewhere afraid of everything.

Grabbing my pen, I jotted down my thoughts before they could flit away. The jittery feeling in my stomach grew as I doodled stars on my paper. You know when you have a great idea and your insides seem to smile back at you? That's how I knew I was onto something.

Now I just needed the perfect medium.

Last year, I'd done an art project that included lots of photos and drawings of my life. Ms. Fenton still has it hanging on the wall in the art room. But this needed to be something even better.

What was the best way to show off all the people who made me *me*?

After school, I couldn't wait to tell Bella and Ashley my awesome plan. Sneaking up on them by the bus lot at the end of the day, I scooped up a handful of snow and launched it at Ashley. Obviously, I made sure to aim for her legs, not her head. I don't have a death wish or anything.

"*Ahh!*" she squealed, whirling around. She searched the crowd with wide eyes. Tiny snowflakes glittered like gems in her hair. Go figure even snowball-attacked Ashley looked like a goddess. "Watch it!" She leaned over, delicately picking up a handful of snow. "I'll get you for that!" She chucked a snowball back at my head.

"Guess what!" I giggled, dodging her attack. Bella ducked out of the way of Ashley's second attempt to snow me as I nearly wiped out on the ice at our feet.

"You're giving up your career as a wildlife nerd to become a figure skater?" Ashley quipped.

"No," I said. "For the media project, I've decided I'm going to talk about *you guys*." I lifted my chin with pride. "I'm going to immortalize you with media! To showcase you with...*something*. I still haven't exactly figured out what kind of media yet. But yeah," I added sheepishly.

Ashley skidded to a stop, sending slush every-where. "For real?" she asked. Her eyelids blinked double-time. "*We* are your influences?"

I nodded. "Yep," I said. "Both of you guys. I don't know what exactly I'm going to do, but I thought it would be cool to talk about how much you guys influence me, you know?" I looked to Bella. "Despite practically never talking for years." I bit my lip. "Or, you know, *hating* each other." I poked Ashley on the shoulder and gave her a fake stink eye.

Bella's hands whipped to her mouth. "Ana! That is so *nice*! I've never been anybody's influence before! That's so cool." She beamed, reaching over to give me a hug.

Ashley was much quieter, but the surprised look on her face was loud enough.

"That's…" she started, looking me up and down. "That's really cool of you, Ana." Her eyes brightened. "I mean it's surprising, but… *Wow*. Who else are you going to talk about?"

Before I could say anything else, my phone buzzed. Mr. Nicholson didn't let us use our phones in class, but my parents always wanted me to keep the ringer on after class every day, in case they needed to get in touch with us. I yanked off my mittens to read the message.

Dazmanian Devil: Where are you? Come home now!

"It's Daz," I moaned. "Five minutes late and he's already being annoying." I glared at the screen and texted back.

AnaBanana: What's your prob? I'll be home soon! It's your turn for chores anyway!

I barely had time to put my mittens back on before he texted again.

Dazmanian Devil: COME HOME, OKAY?! :)

"Sorry, guys," I said, lifting my backpack higher on my shoulder. A smiley face in a text? This can't be good. "I have to run. I'm pretty sure Daz is burning down the house right now."

Chapter 3

Grizzly bears have excellent memory, especially when it comes to remembering where food is buried.

—*Animal Wisdom*

Can't blame them there, right? who doesn't want to remember where they hid the cookies from their brother?

"If Dwayne 'The Rock' Johnson is in my laundry again, I'm going to murder you!" I announced, slamming the front door shut. The house hadn't burned down. Daz was nowhere in sight. In fact, nothing looked weird at all. The warm air inside the house felt like a hug after walking home in the chilly weather.

Kicking off my boots, I tiptoed around the slushy mess at the doorway so my socks didn't get wet. The *only* thing worse than wet boots was wet socks, when you ended up squishing from room to room with cold feet everywhere. Stupid snow.

"I think murder is probably a little extreme," Dad said, peeking out from the kitchen. An old apron was tied around his waist, and he was wielding a wooden spoon stained with something red. "Unless you're going to attack Daz with a murder of *crows*?" He giggled at his own joke.

CREATURE FILE

SPECIES NAME: *Goofballicus Fatheropta*

KINGDOM: Our house, making dinner so Mom doesn't set the kitchen on fire; the gorilla exhibit at the zoo, where he studies them and usually comes home smelling like them too.

PHYLUM: Funny dads with mustaches that twitch when they're thinking hard; excellent hug giver and maker of blanket forts.

WEIGHT: Whatever it is, he's always moaning when he steps on the scale and muttering about treadmills.

FEEDS ON: Family meetings, gorilla stuff, Mom's special pineapple cookies with extra cinnamon sugar on top.

LIFE SPAN: Pretty sure dads are immortal.

HANDLING TECHNIQUE: If you're staying up late to read, make sure that he can see the light underneath your blanket because then he'll leave you alone. Keep a stash of M&M's in the car for long rides because Goofballicus Fatheropta gets *hangry* after a few hours without food.

I gave him a look. "It's Daz's turn to help out, not mine. You can tell him to stop bugging me with his texts!"

"Ten four, peanut! We're making your favorite tonight to celebrate!"

"To celebrate what?" I yelled on the way to my room.

He didn't answer. Instead, a loud clatter of cutlery echoed through the hallway.

"Weirdos," I mumbled, shaking my head. My dad was usually so preoccupied with work, he was in Gori-La La Land half the time. For a second, I debated knocking on Daz's door and chewing him out for his irritating texts. But why wake the beast?

As my hand was on my bedroom doorknob, Daz's door opened. His head poked out of his room like a gopher. That on its own wasn't scary, but the look in his eyes was another story. A devilish grin spread over his face.

"You going in there?" he asked, tapping his door frame aimlessly with his fingertip. He batted his eyelashes. Was it just me or was his hair extra spiky today? I knew from experience, the spikier his hair was, the greater the chance of me being embarrassed.

I took a step back from my door. "*Why?*" I asked. "Why are you asking that?" Whenever Daz got that look in his eyes, the only correct response was to take cover. "Why is everyone acting so weird today? Dad even said we were celebrating something today? Is that what all your texts were about?"

He shook his head, but Daz could have angel wings and be playing the harp on a cloud and he *still* wouldn't look innocent.

"No reason," he said. The mischievous glimmer in his eyes set my teeth on edge. Nodding to my door, he smiled again. "Go ahead. Go on in!"

He might as well have been telling me to hop into a live volcano at this point.

I peeked back at my door, inspecting the knob for any telltale signs of Daz prankery.

Bloodstains?

Nope.

Hidden insects?

Nope.

Superglue?

Nope.

What was he up to?

"You didn't let one of your snakes loose in my room again, did you? I *told* you, I am not going to keep helping you find Oscar if you're dumb enough to set him loose in there."

He giggled and closed his door mysteriously. "Good *luuuuck*," he said from behind the door.

I frowned, giving myself a pep talk. *I will not live in fear of my brother. I will not live in fear of my brother!*

Cracking my door open, I sniffed inside. It might seem weird, but there was no way he was going to get me with a skunk again like the Great Stink of '11.

My room smelled normal from the outside.

But when I yanked my door open, my heart fell into my butt.

"Oh my God," I breathed. My ears began to tingle, and my vision began to do swirly-whirlies. "You're kidding me!" I steadied myself on the door frame as I gaped at her.

It wasn't a reptile staring back at me.

Instead, it was a girl with bright eyes, clunky boots, and fingerless gloves.

A face I hadn't seen in months!

"You're actually here!" I yelped.

Liv—as in, *the* Liv, my lifelong best friend who I hadn't seen since she moved to New Zealand— uncrossed her arms and wiggled her fingers in the air. "*Surpriiiise!*"

Chapter 4

The cougar holds the Guinness World Record for the animal with the most number of names. It is also called puma, mountain lion, panther, catamount, and more, depending on the region.

—*Animal Wisdom*

My friend Liv has a bunch of names too. Olivia. Livi. Livia. Liviola. But the most important thing about Liv? She is here RIGHT NOW.

"What are you doing here?!" I fumbled, kicking my dirty socks out of the way to reach her.

"Is that any way to greet your best friend?" Liv stood up from my bed and scrambled over to me, giving me a giant hug. She smelled like strawberry body spray and licorice.

"Sorry!" I said. "I'm just so surprised to see you! I mean, *look* at you!"

I didn't mean to be staring, but I couldn't help myself. She looked so...different! Not *bad* different, but not at all like the Liv that moved away six months ago. Her face was thinner, like her cheeks had lost their squishiness, and her chin had gotten a bit pointier. A knitted, wooly hat was tugged down over her ears.

When she was here, she used to live in jeans, T-shirts, and cardigans. You know, typical geeky girl stuff. But the girl in front of me was wearing tight black pants, a black long-sleeved shirt layered with a T-shirt from some band I'd never heard of, and a clunky pair of black boots that easily made her two inches taller than me. She looked like the kind of girl that cardigans would run away from in fear. Some sort of inky, dark lip gloss made her teeth look extra-white every time she smiled.

"You're so tall!" I sputtered, stepping back to take another look at her.

And you have chesticles now! I didn't say that part out loud.

She beamed. "Dad said I've grown over an inch since we left. It must be the fresh New Zealand air."

She spun around, yanked off her hat, and twirled around like a ballerina, with her dark purple-streaked hair whipping around her.

Wait.

Purple hair?!

"Whoa!" I said, reaching out to touch a lock of it. "Your parents actually let you dye your hair purple?!" I tried to picture straight-laced, cut-the-crusts-off-your-sandwich Mr. and Mrs. Reed letting Liv do something so outrageous. They wouldn't even let her wear tinted lip gloss until she was twelve!

She grinned. "They didn't *let* me, but it's kind of too late now, isn't it? So awesome, right? Leilani has purple hair too, but hers is more magenta-y, like hot purple. Mine's called Violent Violet," she said, like that explained everything.

I swallowed.

Violent Violet.

My best friend who stops to pick up ladybugs from the side of the road so they don't get stepped on had *Violent Violet* hair.

I'd heard of Leilani before—that's the girl that Liv met when she first moved to New Zealand. I was still trying to get used to hearing her name without cringing. To me, it seemed like she was put on this earth for the sole purpose of yanking away my best friend.

"How long are you here for?" My eyes popped out again as I noticed the ear stud sparkling on the top of her ear. "And what is *that*?!"

"Oh, this?" She tucked her hair (her purple hair!) behind her ear to show off a silvery stud. "It's a dragon." She nudged me with her elbow. "Almost as good as a crocodile, huh, Crocodile Girl?" She winked, but my head was spinning too much to respond.

"*Whoa*," I breathed.

I had to sit down.

Tucking my knees up under me on my bed, I tried to find Liv's old self somewhere behind all the weird.

"You've totally changed too," she said. "You're taller, and your boobs look *awesome*." She nodded gravely.

I snorted, thankful for the new snowman bra Mom had given me a few weeks ago. "So you are the same old Liv after all."

With her sitting in my desk chair with her feet perched on the edge of my bed, it almost felt like old times. So what if her hair was purple and she had a dragon in her ear? She was still Liv, and for the first time since first seeing her in my room, my heart seemed to realize that. A swell of happiness bloomed inside of me.

My best friend is in my room right now.

"So," I started to ask again, "how long can you stay?"

Liv's eyes sparkled with excitement. "Mom and Dad said this trip could be our vacation!" she squealed. "I did awesome at school this semester, even though it's grade nine." She waved her hand flippantly. "And they said this would be a better time anyway, because we're going to do our first Christmas at home when we get back! Pretty cool, right? I'll be here for almost two weeks!"

Two weeks with Liv home!

Instantly my mind whirred with ideas for us; we could have sleepovers and make lip gloss and talk about boys and go see movies and…

She kept babbling. "I mean, I wasn't sure if it was the best time to come here, because there's this great program for drama starting up, and Leilani and I really wanted to get these two parts as sisters in the play, but then I figured I can probably memorize lines while I'm here anyways, so—" She stopped short.

"I'm totally rambling now, aren't I?" she asked suddenly.

I tried to smile. A small twinge of jealously unfurled inside me to hear her talk about Leilani, but this didn't seem like the right time to mention that. Had Liv had the chance to come visit and actually thought she might not *want* to? All because of some play with Leilani?

My stomach twisted.

"No, it's fine," I said, swallowing down the question. "It's great to hear you in person." I smiled gently. It wasn't like *I* didn't have new friends too.

Speaking of which, what exactly was the best way to tell her about Ashley?

I was opening my mouth to speak again when Mom popped her head into my room. "You girls all caught up yet? We're going to eat a little early tonight so Liv can join us." The smell of spicy taco meat and cheesy goodness wafted in behind her.

Liv kicked me gently with her big boot. "You bet, Mrs. Wright! Thanks again for helping me surprise Ana," she said.

"No problem, hun. I was afraid Henry let the cat out of the bag when he said we were celebrating tonight. *Boys*," Mom said, rolling her eyes. "It's so nice to see you two together again, even if it is for a short while. You look so *different!*" She glanced at me, and I could tell she was trying to gauge if I was okay with everything.

And by *everything*, I mean the whole "my best friend is now an alien with purple hair, grungy shirts, and butt-kicking boots" thing.

I smiled at her as breezily as I could muster. I'm sure it came out like a twitchy grin, but another clatter from Dad in the kitchen distracted her. She always says that between the two of them, her and Dad together add up to a pretty good cook.

I beg to disagree.

"Dinner will be ready in five minutes, okay?" She darted back into the hallway. "Make sure you wash up."

"So," Daz said, shoveling half a taco into his mouth. "What's the coolest thing about living in New Zealand?"

"Daz," Mom warned. "Please eat like a civilized person, especially when we have guests." She dabbed a glob of salsa onto her plate and sprinkled cheese onto her taco.

Daz's face screwed up, and he looked to Dad for backup. "Since when is Liv a *guest*?" he asked. Strings of lettuce and cheese dangled from his chin like worms, and there was a glob of what appeared to be guacamole on his temple. At least, I hoped it was guacamole, because if not, Daz was likely contagious by now.

"Liv used to eat here practically every week before she moved away," he pointed out.

He was right about that. But still, there was something sort of...*weird* about having her sitting next to me at the dinner table now. Was it the strange clothes or the hair? Usually, I gobbled down my dinner without coming up for air, but now I felt like I was trying to sit a little taller than normal and take smaller, measured bites. Why didn't it feel like it always did when she came over for dinner before she moved away?

"Hey!" Daz interrupted again. "Have you been hearing about stuff here while you were gone?" He pointed his fork at me accusingly and waggled his eyebrows. A tense knot tightened in my stomach.

Liv perked up. "I know Ana did that crocodile presentation when the summer started!" she chimed. "Last I heard"—she turned to me—"your grandpa was working at that aquarium thingy?"

Daz erupted with laughter. "You should have seen Ana on opening day!" He wiped his hands on a napkin and licked his fingers, giggling at me. "Did you tell her about what happened with the shark tank? When you were trying to stop—"

"Hey!" I half yelled, half coughed while I kicked him under the table. Mom peered over at me with all sorts of unasked questions in her eyes.

Okay, so I didn't exactly tell Liv a lot about last summer, including my little dip in the shark tank. But that's only because I didn't know how to bring it up without mentioning the whole Ashley thing.

The truth was, I didn't want to spill the beans about Ashley—and the fact that we were actually *friends* now—in front of my whole family. That's the sort of thing that you mention when you're together alone.

Preferably with ice-cream sundaes to soften the blow.

I *knew* Liv would flip when she heard it, and giving her time to adjust to the news was the *nice* thing to do. The best friend thing to do. I owed her that.

"Liv didn't answer your first question," I blurted, trying to cover my tracks.

I glared at Daz, trying to send him all of this telepathically. He shrugged and stuffed another taco into his mouth. I could always count on carbs to shut him up.

"So," I said calmly, "what *is* the best part about New Zealand?"

Liv chewed her bite slowly, tapping her chin with her finger as she thought. She did the same thing during tests at school, only instead of her finger, she taps her pencil. It was über-weird seeing her do all the same things like chin-tapping when she looked so incredibly different.

"The people are so fun," she said finally. "I mean, the scenery is, like, the most gorgeous stuff on the planet, and there are all these mountains and amazing beaches everywhere…"

"There are loads of mountains here," Daz pointed out, slurping salsa from the side of his mouth.

"True," she said. "But these mountains are different, I guess." She turned to Mom. "Did you guys know there are no snakes in New Zealand?"

I narrowed my eyes. "Seriously? Like, none?" I tried to picture a life without snakes. In my world, that would pretty much be a life without air. A whole country without snakes?

Dad wiped his mustache with his napkin. "It's true, kiddo. They also don't have any large mammal predators. No bears, wolves...nada," he explained.

I slumped down in my chair. "That doesn't sound very interesting," I said. I didn't mean to sound like a snob, but come on now. No predators? Where was the excitement in that?

Liv shook her head. "But it's so beautiful! And sometimes they don't give you bills at your table when you go to a restaurant!"

I chewed another bite of taco. "How does that work?"

Daz jumped in. "Do you get to dine and dash?" he asked, his eyes widening.

Liv giggled, tucking some of her purple hair behind her ear. "No," she said. "I mean, you *could*, I guess. People are a lot more trusting there, I think. When you're done with your meal, you go up to the cash register yourself and tell them what you had and then you pay there."

Mom smiled. "That's very interesting, Liv. That will come in handy if we ever get to visit you there." She dunked her neatly wrapped taco into the salsa on her plate and followed it with sour cream.

"Yup," she said. I could tell by the way she was puffing up and grinning that she loved talking about her new home. My stomach clenched even tighter. "*And* there is only one native mammal species," she added, nodding at me. "I looked that up for *you*. It was some teensy little bat creature that was as small as my thumb."

Maybe it was the taco meat doing a number on my tummy, or maybe all this "Yay, New Zealand!" talk was making me edgy. I don't remember Liv talking about her old home here like this. Had she forgotten about life here in only six months?

Mom seemed to sense the shift at the table. "And how about school? Are you enjoying it? What's your favorite class?"

Liv smiled tightly, wiping sour cream from her lip. "High school is great!" she said, keeping her eyes down to stuff some more cheese into her taco. "I mean, it's not like school here, but that's okay." Her face brightened as she spoke. "I was super worried I wasn't going to make any friends, but I met Leilani—she's the girl I was telling you about earlier." She gestured to me. "She is the *best*. And since then, she's introduced me to loads of people."

I squirmed at the word *best*, which seemed to slither inside my heart like a viper ready to strike. *Best* was too close to *best friend* for my liking. Had Liv really changed so much she could be best-anythings with someone with purple hair?

"As for classes." She tapped her chin again, interrupting my panic. "I love drama. I thought about joining the math club when I got there, but the kids in drama are *so* crazy! I'm not sure if math club would be as much fun. They're sorta geeky," she said.

I nearly dropped my taco. Liv, calling the math kids *geeky*?! She had been one of the cochairs of the Algebrainiacs at school last year. And now she's worried about geeky?

"It's so much fun, Ana," she added. "They're hilarious!"

There was a weird lilt to her voice that seemed off-kilter, but her face remained perma-grinny when I peeked up at her. You know when you're getting your picture taken and the person with the camera takes *forever* so your smile starts to hurt and feel all shaky and crumbly on your face, and you know you look like a total weirdo? *That* is the kind of smile Liv gave me.

It gave me the creeps.

Of course, my parents were too occupied with telling Daz to stop making a salsa volcano out of his leftovers to notice that.

"Hey," I said. I could feel the tug of desperation behind my words, but I had to do *something* to get rid of this squicky-Leilani feeling inside of me. "I have a great idea!" I don't know why I hadn't thought of it before. "We should go to Shaken, Not Stirred now that you're back! *Just* the two of us!" I darted a look at Daz, who never missed an opportunity for whipped cream calories.

Liv grinned, but this time it was a real one. "That sounds great! We can celebrate me being here!" She lifted her fork and waved it like a tiny flag. "Mom and Dad have a whole bunch of relatives they want to see while we're here, but we can go tomorrow!"

"Perfect!" I said, glancing to my parents for their approval. Mom nodded, and I could see she was proud of me for not being a pill about the whole "no mammals" thing earlier. "We can celebrate your visit and hang out like old times," I said.

Like old times when you *didn't* seem like a stranger with purple hair.

Chapter 5

The color of an ermine's coat changes throughout the year. In warmer months, it is a rich brown. In the wintertime, it becomes snowy white.

—*Animal Wisdom*

How useful would this be, right?! Instead of worrying about what to wear every single morning so people don't realize I'm a complete fashion disaster, I could wear the same thing all through the hot months, and then switch over to winter mode when the snow came. Ermines have all the luck.

The next day, I couldn't shake the strange feeling in my stomach. At first, I thought it was the mountain of tacos we'd eaten, but the more I thought about it, the more I realized that I was pretty messed up about some of the things that Liv had said at dinner. *So* messed up, in fact, that I didn't technically tell anyone about Liv being here the next day at school and came up with some lame excuse about having to clean my room tonight instead of hanging out with anyone.

I know. I'm a terrible friend. But it wasn't like Ashley or Bella *had* to know that second that Liv was here for a visit. They barely even knew her! And okay, it's also true that every time I thought of Liv, I had this image of Leilani in my head that kept popping up like a rodent in one of those Whac-a-Mole games. All night long, I'd even dreamed of Liv and Leilani starring in some Broadway play together, with their name in bright lights. Newspapers were printed with giant headlines in my dream, splashing our names across the page:

Leilani Replaces Ana as Liv's New Best Friend! Liv and Leilani Set to Appear in Broadway Musical: The Violent Violet Sisters! Buy Tickets Now!

Thanks for nothing, brain.

How come one stupid move to the other side of the planet could make two friends feel so weird around each other? Or maybe it was just *me*, because so far, Liv hadn't said anything about feeling off. Either way, I was determined to forget how strange things felt and get back to normal. Grandpa has this saying, about how you can't control fate, but you *can* lend it a hand every so often. Now, I don't know if fate is the reason that Liv was acting like a different person, but I had to do my part to make sure that we stayed best friends.

No matter what country she lived in.

I knew that if I was going to get things back to normal between us, I would probably have to jog her memory and tug her away from all the new stuff in her life. Namely, Leilani and hobbits and all that. Not to mention the purple hair.

Before showing up that afternoon at the Shaken, Not Stirred ice-cream shop after school, I made sure to wear the tie-dyed shirt we'd made for my eleventh birthday party and the sneakers with the blue laces she'd given me for Christmas the following year. Every time I looked at those laces, I remembered that day and how she came over for Christmas breakfast early with us and filled up on croissants and fruit salad, then we went back to her house and did the whole thing again. Friends did that kind of thing, and I was positive that she would have the exact same memory when she saw them. Then we could order our shakes (she would get cherry), and we could get back to normal.

I took a deep breath and shoved open the door.

Liv was sitting cross-legged in a booth. A smile spread over my face when I saw it was the *same* booth we always used to sit in together. See? She remembered everything, just like me.

"Hey!" I said, plunking down across from her in the booth. She set the menu down on the table, and her jaw dropped.

"Oh my *God*!" she squealed as I unzipped my coat and unwound the fuzzy scarf from my neck. "Is that the shirt from your birthday party?" Her eyes darted around us.

I wriggled my shoulders proudly. "Sure is! Remember when we made them? You got green dye all over your fingers and under your nails. It took weeks to come off." I giggled. "And check out these laces!"

I stuck out my foot so she could see the bright-blue laces on my sneakers. Although my feet were *freezing* in this chilly weather, it was totally worth the frostbite for the laces.

Liv made a face. "I do remember it, but wow, Ana. It looks *bad*. You look like a ten-year-old! It barely fits!"

A fizz of heat ran through my body. "I do not!" I

said, slumping down. The way Liv was glancing all around made me wary of who was looking at us. Or more specifically, *me*. But who cared? I was wearing a shirt from my *best friend*—that should mean something.

Even if it was hideous.

"I thought you would like it," I mumbled. "I don't wear it all the time or anything," I added hotly.

She laughed. "Well, that's good! You know there are lots of great YouTube videos about style now? I got into them when we moved, and they have been *s-o-o-o* helpful." She picked up the menu again. "I can't believe some of the things we used to wear," she said lightly. "That shirt is one thing, but remember those matching hats we had all through third grade? God, what was *wrong* with us?"

I frowned. I had looked for that hat this morning to add to my "friendship ensemble," but couldn't find it in my disaster of a closet.

Was it me or was she now pretty much hiding behind the stupid menu? *Nothing* was wrong with us. We were friends, and sometimes friends wore silly things together. That was the whole point: the *together* part. Even the dumb things are fun when you're doing it with friends.

I forced myself not to slouch. "I wanted to wear something that reminded me of you," I said.

Of us, I added to myself.

57

Liv's face softened, and her eyes scrunched up with a smile. "Is it weird that I sort of love that those goofy shoes and horrible shirts remind you of me?"

My heart lifted. "See! They still *fit*." I squirmed in my top. "Okay, not really," I admitted.

Liv leaned closer to me, lowering her voice. "Do you remember that time we wore those pink tutus from Goodwill to school in second grade because we thought it would convince our fairy godmothers to find us?" She shook her head gravely.

"I can't believe they didn't show up," I said, cackling at Liv's fake-disgusted face.

As Lacey the waitress sidled up to our booth, we tried to pull ourselves together. This was more like it! We were two best friends who were a little out of sync at first. Now, the twisty nervous feeling in my stomach was fading.

"Hello, girls," Lacey drawled. Pulling the pencil from behind her ear, she blinked at us over her notepad. "What can I get ya?"

"A vanilla shake please, extra whipped cream and two cherries!" I announced.

Liv pursed her lips, tapping her chin. "I'll have the…"

"Oh! Ana! Wait!" Lacey interrupted, sticking her pen in her hair. "Sorry, hun." She apologized to Liv and turned back to face me. "I completely forgot to tell you, my niece was watching the news last week and saw some little advertisement for the zoo with you in it and flipped her *lid* when I told her I knew you! Would you mind signing a copy of your grandpa's book for her? We got a copy when he was here last, and I know I'd be the best aunt ever if I gave it to her with your signature!"

My chest tightened. In all my life, someone asking for my autograph was about the craziest thing I think I would ever expect. Crazier than zombie sloths taking over the streets. Crazier than Daz enrolling in beauty school. Crazier than—

"I have it here! In the back!" Lacey blurted. "You and your friends are in here a lot, so I knew you'd be in soon enough. Is that okay?"

I glanced at Liv, unable to keep the excitement off my face. This was kind of cool! And incredibly *nuts*. "Um…I guess so?" But Lacey had already bustled off to the kitchen for the book.

Liv kept her eyes down to her menu as Lacey returned with Grandpa's hardcover in her hands. "Thank you so much!" she exclaimed. "She'll love it. Her name is Olivia."

"Oh! That's her name too!" I pointed to Liv. "Two Olivias!" I took the book from her hands. What was I supposed to write? Do I just sign my name? Should I do a little drawing? For a second, I looked up to Liv for advice, but she was searching in her purse for lip gloss. She smeared the inky darkness over her lips as I looped my signature on the title page. I added a little smiley face for good measure, along with a "I think you're great!" message.

Lacey grinned at Liv. "Have you lived here long? I don't remember seeing you here." She chatted animatedly, but Liv was still sitting there with a tight smile on her face.

"Liv was here her whole life until she moved to New Zealand before the summer!" I explained, trying to stop the icy feeling that was spreading around me. I had to admit, this whole "sign an autograph in front of your long-lost best friend" was a teensy bit weird. "You probably don't recognize her because her hair is purple now," I added.

Lacey nodded. "Cool. And thanks so much for this, Ana!" She took the book and stuffed it into her apron pocket, then found her notepad again. "Sorry, what did you guys want again?"

I took a deep breath, secretly feeling super proud of myself for not botching that autograph by spelling my name wrong. "A vanilla shake, with extra whipped cream and two cherries," I said. I pointed to Liv for her to order.

Cherry shake with extra sprinkles, I thought triumphantly.

"Toffee crunch swirl sundae," she said finally. "Please." She handed the menu to Lacey, who nodded and bustled back to the counter.

"No cherry shake?" I tried to mask my surprise with a laugh, but it came out more like a hacky, super-surprised cough.

She shrugged. "The toffee crunch looked good too," she said. Something about the way she was holding her smile made me nervous again. She wasn't even looking me in the eyes anymore, and her dark lip gloss made her look like a storm cloud. When you've known someone forever, you can instantly tell when they're acting weird. And this was *weird*, no matter how Liv tried to hide it.

"You've never gotten one before, in all the years you lived here," I said, keeping my voice light. "Is everything okay? If this is about the book—"

"What?" she snapped. "Because I want to try something new?" There was an edge to her voice that made me flinch. She must have noticed because she rolled her eyes and scoffed.

"I'm fine. Okay?" She shook her head. "So. Tell me *everything*."

I blinked. "Everything what?" The shift from weird-Liv to normal again was enough to give me whiplash.

She tsked. "You know, *everything* everything. I haven't seen you in months! You have to catch me up on everything that we couldn't talk about over dinner! How is Kevin? How is school? How are the awful Sneerers? Has Ashley self-imploded from sneeriness yet or what?"

Suddenly my tongue felt too big for my mouth. Now was the perfect time to tell her that the Sneerers and I, well, *one* Sneerer in particular, were actually friends now. It would be a great way to show Liv that she wasn't the only one changing.

But what if I told her and things got even *weirder* between us? I didn't want to risk her getting snippy again, did I? Maybe now wasn't the best time.

I snapped back to reality. "Kevin's good. We've been going out since the start of school. Mom lets us go on group dates mostly, which is pretty cool. With Bella and Daz, I mean."

Liv's eyebrows lifted. "Is that the shy girl with the weird pixie cut? The one who was always buried behind some book in class?" Her tone wasn't mean, but my skin crawled uncomfortably at how she described Bella.

"Yeah," I said. "Well. No," I corrected. "She was, *is*, super shy, but she's actually supercool and smart. I like her hair too…" I trailed off awkwardly. I wasn't trying to defend Bella or anything, because Liv didn't mean it as an insult. But still.

She nodded, smushing her dark-stained lips

together. "So you go on group dates with Kevin, and you still haven't kissed him yet? How come?!" Her mouth drooped into a phony, mopey frown. "You left me all by my lonesome on our kiss pact. Hmph." Her voice turned all gloopy, like she was sad.

I clenched my hand into a fist. I *hated* whenever Liv brought up the kiss pact. See, if I rewind a bit, we made a deal back when we were little kids that we would kiss a boy (a different boy, obviously) before we went to high school. But *then*, Liv went and skipped a grade, which turned our kiss pact into a nightmare. Ashley and Bella knew the story, but for some reason, admitting everything to Liv felt like admitting defeat. Like she was some grown-up, while I was still a loser kid.

Which made no sense, because it wasn't even something *I* wanted.

Since when did Liv make me feel so…*immature*?

"Hey!" I blurted, eager to change the subject. A bright, flickering idea gave me the perfect way to get our conversation back on track and hopefully stop Liv from doing that angry-smushing thing with her mouth. "I'm doing this media project at school, and I'd like to profile you! As one of my influences, I mean," I said. "It's all about the people that influence us. Cool, huh?"

"Do I have to do anything special?" she asked, suddenly looking nervous.

I shook my head. "Nope. You can help me whenever I figure out what kind of medium I want to use. I *have* to include my best friend, of course."

Liv smiled, but there was something missing behind her eyes. "That's cool. Let me know if I can help," she said, chewing her lip. "Oh! Did you want to see a picture of Ryan?" She reached back for her purse.

"Ryan's the guy you like, right?" I leaned forward to see the picture she was finding on her phone.

She nodded. "He's *so* cute." She held it out.

A boy with a snarly look on his face glared at whoever was taking the photo. His hair was dark and a little too long, like he hadn't gotten it cut in time for pictures like most kids. He didn't look cute to me, but I wasn't about to say that to Liv. He looked like the kind of guy I'd cross the street to avoid. She held the phone to her chest and sighed, all dramatic-like.

"We aren't going *out*, going out. Yet. But Leilani said that he told his brother Max that he liked me, so that has to count, right?" She bit her lip and stared at me.

"Right!" I said. "He looks...uh..."

Scary.

Greasy.

Murdery.

"Cool," I said finally. "He looks pretty old for his age, actually," I added, inspecting the picture again.

"He's in ninth grade with me, so that makes him a year older. He turns fourteen in a few months!" She giggled.

Fourteen.

If there was anything scarier sounding than thirteen, it was fourteen. But I guess if Liv was technically in ninth grade now, she would always be hanging out with older kids, right? Did that make me one of her "younger" friends?

I didn't like the sound of that.

Suddenly I felt a little dumb for wearing this stupid shirt, like I was proving to her even more that I was a little kid. Why hadn't I thought of that *before* I'd picked my outfit?

I shifted until I was sitting on my feet, tucking the blue laces out of sight. And then, the weirdest, craziest thing happened.

I wasn't expecting it.

I couldn't stop it.

For the first time in a decade of best friendship with Liv, a silence grew between us.

And I don't mean a quiet type of silence, where everyone takes a minute to have a drink or check their teeth for spinach.

No. I would have been okay with that.

Those types of silences are normal.

This was an *awkward* type of silence, when both people end up catching each other's eyes and they *know* someone needs to say something, but absolutely nothing comes out because you can't think of a *thing* to say and you get that squirmy feeling in your guts like you want to shrink down and fly away like a bug. When the whole world gets swallowed up by how downright quiet everything is.

My stomach dropped, like I'd swan dived off a cliff.

Liv cleared her throat.

The seconds on the wall clock ticked by... s-l-o-w-l-y...like they were counting down the last seconds of our friendship, as it was going to be washed away for good. Panic clawed at me.

Say something already!

"And here you go!" Lacey's perky voice interrupted the gigantic hole of nothingness between us. She set my vanilla shake in front of me and slid Liv's mess of toffee and whipped cream to her.

I unwrapped my straw. Could Lacey tell that there was currently a black hole floating in the middle of our booth? It probably had its own gravitational pull by now, sucking our friendship in like a Hoover.

As Lacey walked away, I scrambled for something to say before that horrible quiet took over the booth again, but Liv beat me to it.

"So are you glad you're not living in the zoo anymore?" she asked. She swirled a clump of toffee in with her ice cream and licked the spoon. "Mmm. I haven't had ice cream in so long," she swooned.

"It ended up being pretty fun, actually. Mom says we'll probably get to move back in next summer for more of her research." A buzz of adrenaline swam through me as I connected the dots. This was the perfect chance to tell Liv about Ashley, before she found out on her own. I tried to think of the best way to bring it up.

Tell her already. Now, while she's got ice cream!

"Grandpa opened up this cool aquarium exhibit during the summer, and they said that a whole bunch of students wanted to help out," I started.

Liv smacked her lips on another bite, nodding.

"All because of you, I bet." She narrowed her eyes at me. There was a sharp tone to her voice, even though her words were airy. "You got all famous with that crocodile thing, and now everyone wants to be like you! When is that documentary of your grandpa's going to be finished, you think?"

"Not for a long time, maybe like next summer," I said casually, trying not to sound uppity about it. I didn't want Liv thinking I'd become some *diva*, especially since it's pretty much physically impossible to be a diva when your claim to fame is crocodile poop. And that's with or without people asking for your autograph.

I focused on the two cherries sitting on the top of my shake. For a moment, I wondered if they were also best friends. Did one cherry ever have some weird, awkward silence with the other while they were hanging out?

I went on, before I could lose my nerve. "About the aquarium," I said, thinking of the best way to work Ashley into the story. "Some kids from our school showed up to help too. I was surprised at first, but we ended up being really good friends. You're not going to believe it, but one of them was—"

A loud chime interrupted me. Liv's eyes brightened as she stuck her spoon back in her ice cream and scrambled for her purse. She snorted loudly as she pulled out her phone and read the screen.

"Oh my God, Leilani is the *funniest*," she said absently. Her fingers raced along the keyboard of her phone as she giggled.

"Ashley," I muttered.

You'd think that Liv would have dropped her phone and acted completely surprised when I mentioned Ashley, right? Maybe ask me how on earth I'd coped working with Ashley at the zoo. That's what a real friend would do, right?

But nope.

Liv didn't do any of those things because she was too busy texting someone else.

Her *other* friend.

She turned the phone to me, showing me the screen. "Check it out," she said. "She dyed some of her bangs *green* with a Magic Marker! It looks so great!"

I stared at the picture. It was the first time I'd ever seen Leilani, and I don't know what I was expecting. Maybe a supermodel? Or a robot with dead-shark eyes that stared through me as they stole away my best friend?

But she just looked like a girl with messed-up purple-and-green hair. Mom would have *killed* me if I'd tried a stunt like that! To be honest, she looked like a kid that got sent to the principal's office for saying bad words to the teacher.

I avoided her eyes.

"I have to get back soon," I fumbled, shoving the last third of my shake away from me. A greasy, slimy feeling crawled over me like a wet snake. "I promised Mom I'd help her at the zoo tonight," I lied.

Liv grabbed her purse and swung it under her arm. "Okay," she said. "What were you saying about Ashley again?"

I shook my head, feeling my shake rumbling dangerously close to my throat. "Nothing. She's still a giant Sneerer," I said, shrugging. The words popped out of my mouth without warning.

I hadn't meant to lie. Or had I?

Chapter 6

Bighorn sheep have four-chambered stomachs. To eat, they regurgitate their food (called "cud") and then re-swallow it for further digestion.

—*Animal Wisdom*

The word *regurgitate* should be outlawed. Just saying. (Along with the words *puberty*, *training bra*, and *hallway monitor*. Nobody needs any of those.)

Who wears high heels and always has perfect hair?

No, it's not the start of a lame joke, but it *is* the truth about Grandpa's girlfriend, Sugar.

There are two things you should know about Grandpa and Sugar.

1. They are both so stinkin' famous that they can barely go out the door without someone jamming a camera in their faces, hoping for a million-dollar moment they can sell to some tabloid. Grandpa is famous because he's a super-popular naturalist and reality TV star. Seriously, he films documentaries where he wears bandanas and eats worms and all that. Sugar, on the other hand, is his supermodel girlfriend with perfect hair, manicured toes, and a stomach like those ladies on the magazines at the checkout. That's pretty much enough of a reason to be famous these days, but she's so nice too. She's a lot younger than Grandpa, but the more I hang out with him, the more I realize he's actually a twenty-year-old trapped in an old guy's body.

2. After three months of living in Los Angeles again, they were super eager to visit us. Even if Mom put them to work doing yard cleanup.

"Daz!" Mom shouted. "Your job is to pick up all the branches and twigs from the tree, not climb the actual tree!" She shielded her eyes from the sun as she gawked up at him. Daz swung down a branch and let his feet dangle. I wasn't surprised he was so good at climbing trees and swinging on branches. Most monkeys are, after all.

Grandpa tossed a pebble at him from below. "Get down here and help out your grandpa, young man! I'm too old for this!" His tone was serious, but I could see the trademark sparkle in his eyes as he twirled around his rake in a graceful move like the guy from *Singin' in the Rain* on the lamppost.

CREATURE FILE

SPECIES NAME: *Shep Spotlighticus*

KINGDOM: The whole world! *Shep Spotlighticus* thrives in any environment, due to his crazy charisma and ability to make anyone laugh while teaching them about weird animals.

PHYLUM: Grandfathers who also happen to be naturalists featured on bimonthly tabloids, *Entertainment Now's* #5 Most Eligible Bachelor; after that, good-looking news anchor guy, that British actor with the voice like butter that everyone's always swooning over, and two football players. (Sugar hates that he's called a "bachelor" by the way, because they've been dating for a while now. Just saying.)

WEIGHT: "Shipshape for his age" (so he says).

FEEDS ON: Dangerous situations where he's up against venomous snakes, stinging insects, or snapping jaws; also spaghetti.

LIFE SPAN: I think he has nine lives, like a cat.

HANDLING TECHNIQUE: None needed. Loves to hang out and laugh and carries candy in his coat pocket.

Beside him, Sugar had swapped her usual high heels for a pair of oversized boots. She looked like she belonged on the cover of a "glamping" magazine, where people camp out in glamorous RVs instead of tents like normal people.

"It's so nice to get out and get some fresh air!" she said, reaching over to grab a handful of broken twigs from one of our windy storms last week. "LA has been suffocating lately. I miss this Denver air!" She took a huge breath, sighing loudly and tipping her tanned face to the sun.

"Enjoy it while you can, Sugar," Dad said. "Knowing the weather around here, it will snow any minute!"

I squinted into the sun as I kicked the last of my own twig pile together. "Done!" I turned to see if I'd beaten Dad in our yearly cleanup race.

He tipped his ball cap at me and scooped some of his leaves with his rake, flinging them in the air. "You got me this time, peanut!" he said, bowing regally. "Why can't your brother get through chores that quickly?"

I grinned, propped the big paper yard waste bag against a tree, and settled at the picnic table with my notebook. The weight of any unfinished project felt heavy on my shoulders, but after my horrible meet up with Liv, it seemed even more important that I thought of the perfect way to do it. I wished that instead of a crabapple tree, we had a great idea tree. Then I could pluck ideas off whenever I needed one.

"What you got there?" Grandpa asked, sidling up next to me on the picnic table bench. He reached over to pour some of the cocoa from Mom's thermos into a mug. "Some of your sketches?" He peeked over at my notes.

"It's for a school project, actually," I said. I handed him my project outline from Mr. Nicholson. "We've got to showcase five things that influence us using a form of media, like a record of what made us who we are in eighth grade. You know, like people and places and stuff." I giggled at the cocoa mustache that had formed on his upper lip. "You're on the list, by the way." I pointed out his name, beside Liv, Ashley, and Bella. "And as for places, I had to include the zoo."

His mouth dropped open. "Me?" He wrapped his flannelly arm around me. "I'm one of your biggest influences? Banana, I'm *honored*!" He lifted his sleeve to his eye, sniffling once.

I squirmed. Something about making your grandpa tear up was a bit too much emotion for yard-work day. But still, it was kind of nice that he cared that much, you know?

"Of course," I said. "You were one of the reasons I got…" I struggled for the right word to sum up how much bigger my life had gotten in such a short time. I had wanted to keep people from knowing we were even *related*, but now that seemed like a million years ago. "Braver," I said finally. "I'm braver because of you."

He sniffed. "Ditto." He nudged me and eyed the rest of my list. "Liv is your friend that moved, right?" He tapped her name on the page.

"Yep," I said, my chest tightening. The image of her giggling over Leilani's messages flashed in my head. "She's visiting, and we've been kind of weird since she got here. I really want to show her she's still my best friend, and I need the perfect way to do it. I want to do something *different*. Something nobody else will do," I said, handing him a napkin for his cocoa mustache from the snack tray Mom had set out for us.

"Hmm…" he said, flipping the page over for Mr. Nicholson's list of potential media we could use. "Some of these are pretty boring, huh? A *blog post essay*?" He made a face. "I never did like writing essays in school," he said, taking another sip of cocoa. "I always got too distracted by all the birds out the window to write more than a sentence or two."

"Sounds like you." I smirked. I couldn't picture Grandpa as a kid like me, stuck in a classroom. He seemed built for the outdoors, surrounded by scary animals. Sometimes I wondered if he was actually raised by wolves, instead of human parents. That might have explained his shaggy hair and tendency to bear his teeth at Daz when he tried to sneak candy from his coat pocket without asking.

"How about a documentary?" Grandpa asked. "That must run in your blood by now, kiddo!" He chuckled, breaking a granola bar in half and tossing it into the air to catch it in his mouth.

I narrowed my eyes. "Does that count?" I checked the list. Sure enough, under the list of film media, there it was.

"Huh," I said, tapping my pencil next to the entry. "I must have skimmed right over that. It sounds kind of…meh," I said.

Grandpa hacked on his granola bar. "Young lady!" He faked a shocked look, his cheeks turning rosy red. "The documentary is *the* single greatest invention of humankind!" He snatched the paper from me and stood up dramatically, gesturing wildly.

I settled back to watch him. Whenever Grandpa got all jazz hands like this it was always pretty entertaining.

"*The* greatest invention?" I questioned. "What about toilet paper? Or Personal Pan Pizzas? Or tranquilizer darts?" I thought about all those times I'd watched Grandpa's documentaries where he was helping relocate large predators, where the only thing between him and a set of snapping jaws was a teensy dart that calmed the animal down.

He pointed at me. "Yes! Those are all wonderful things! Not a day goes by when I'm not grateful for the brilliance of the human mind for such inventions as the Personal Pan Pizza!" He was getting going now, his eyes twinkling like Mom's when she's in front of a crowd.

"But documentaries, my dear Ana banana, are even better, providing a window into amazing worlds—*real* worlds with real creatures that people would never see otherwise! Now *that* is a noble pursuit! To teach *and* entertain? What could be better?"

I giggled. "It is noble. But for this project I'm only going to be showcasing a few people and the zoo," I said. "You know. Nothing wild like anacondas or sharks or things that can carry people off and eat them. Aren't documentaries supposed to be"—I searched for the word—"exciting?"

He lifted his shoulders. "What could be more exciting than a real documentarian glimpse into *your* world? You could be showcasing your influences in *real* time! You could *film* them! You could show them as they've never been seen before—their truest, grittiest, honest selves! If you can tell me that wouldn't be the coolest project in your class, then I will eat my shorts!"

Laughing, I took the paper from him. I didn't tell him that I was sold on the documentary idea the second he'd found it on the list. Truthfully, I was surprised I hadn't thought of it before. I *did* have some experience with documentaries, especially being around Grandpa so much. That familiar warm tingle of excitement ran up my arms, despite the chill in the air.

"You know," I said, playing along. "I think that's the *perfect* idea!"

Instantly, my mind buzzed into action as I started rambling to Grandpa. "I could interview and film everyone, and profile all the things about them that make them who *they* are, which would also show how they influence *me*! It's brilliant!" I high-fived him.

Daz bounded over to the picnic table. Leaves were scattered through his spiky hair at odd angles, so he looked like a doofy scarecrow.

"What's brilliant?" he asked, plunking down across from us. He tried to imitate Grandpa by throwing some granola in the air and catching it, but it bounced off his ear instead and onto the grass.

"Only the most awesome school project *ever*," I said proudly.

Daz's lip curled as he chewed. "You get way too excited about school," he said.

"But think of it!" I continued talking to Grandpa, ignoring Daz's attempt to stuff as many marshmallows as possible into his mug of cocoa. "I could even bring the camera into the zoo!" The idea zapped me like an electric eel. "I bet nobody will do a project like that. Do you think I could borrow a video camera, Grandpa?" I asked. "The only problem is I have no idea how to use a video camera. *Or* how to do any of that fancy editing stuff? Don't you need special programs for that?"

My shoulders drooped. Suddenly my awesome idea felt like Mount Everest, impossible to scale in such a short time.

"I think I know a certain someone who might be able to help you out there." Grandpa's eyebrows lifted mischievously. "Someone who has plenty of experience working with cameras *and* editing software…"

"Woo?" Daz mumbled through his chubby, marshmallow-stuffed cheeks.

"You?" I guessed, translating Daz's marshmallow talk.

"Nope." Grandpa shook his head. "Someone

even better! Sugar! We need your help with a very urgent homework matter!"

Sugar skipped over to us, dancing around in her rain boots.

"Urgent homework matters?!" Her perfectly made-up eyes widened with fear. "Fair warning—I've never liked math." She wrung her hands together, with her pumpkin-orange nails sparkling in the sunlight.

Grandpa smiled. "Ana wants to make a documentary for a project, to profile her influences. Think you could lend her a hand?"

"You?" My jaw dropped. "I mean." I struggled to save face to not hurt Sugar's feelings. She *was* super nice, after all. But homework help? "I assumed you were always a model, so you probably were good at being in *front* of a camera. Not…behind it?"

Sugar batted her lashes. "It's true that I got into modeling, but that wasn't until I'd spent years behind the camera, doll." She puffed up her already ample chest, practically giving Daz a coronary. "I went to school for filmmaking," she said. "I've even been helping produce Shep's latest documentary."

Mom, who had come over for a drink of water, stared at Sugar as she spoke. I could tell by her surprised face that she hadn't expected that one either.

"Wow!" I said. "Would you mind helping me

then? I want to film everybody, and I'll need help with the camera and editing, and it needs to be done pretty quick—"

Sugar lifted her hand. "Ana doll, you're going to have the best documentary that school has ever seen! We can start right away!"

I gave her my media handout as she took a seat at the picnic table to read it. I had to hand it to Sugar. Mom and Dad were irked when they'd met her for the first time because she's loads younger than Grandpa. And yeah, okay, I had been too. But Sugar actually *did* fit into our family. Like, one time, Dad made me a hot cocoa with a teensy pinch of chili powder in it. I thought it would be super weird, but it was *so* good. That one little pinch of chili made it taste that much better. Maybe Sugar was like the pinch of chili powder in our family. She's unexpected, but she sure brought out the flavor in us, you know?

Chapter 7

Despite spending years away, salmon return
to the rivers in which they were born to spawn.
—*Animal Wisdom*

How do they know how to do this?! Is some little corner store under the ocean selling salmon maps? Do they have an app? I get lost on the way to the gym sometimes, so how are they finding home from thousands of miles away?

CLICK.

Late that night, a sudden noise—a *loud* noise—jolted me out of sleep, making my heart hammer in my ears.

"Huh?" I lurched up in bed, blinking at the inky

darkness of my room. Darwin's cage was still covered, so the noise hadn't come from him. Go figure something always has to wake you up when you're having an amazing dream of being at the Academy Awards with Ryan Gosling.

I tugged my comforter closer to my chin as something in the hallway clattered. What was going on out there? Was it Daz? Chills ran up my spine as I peeked at my bedside clock. The time—twelve forty-two in the morning—flashed in neon red.

Click.

There it was again.

Were we being *robbed*?

I snuck from my bed, stepping on the tips of my toes to avoid all the creaky spots in the floor. Opening my door the teensiest crack, I peered down the hallway to see if Daz's door was open. It wouldn't be the first time Daz got up to no good in the middle of the night.

But Daz's door was shut tightly. Shadows and light from the living room window swayed and twisted on the wall like ghosts.

I inhaled sharply, gripping my doorknob tighter. Should I go look? Or was that the first thing that a murderer would expect? How could I get my parents' attention without alerting whoever, or *whatever*, was inside?! In movies the first person to get axed is the idiot girl who goes out and asks who's there.

I didn't have time to decide.

"Ana!" A sharp voice cut through the darkness. I nearly jumped out of my skin. Mom appeared out of nowhere in the hallway, buttoning up the top button on her khaki work shirt.

"Mom!" I clutched my chest, checking that I still had a pulse. "What's going on? I heard noises..."

"Everything's okay," she said in a rough voice. Her hair was piled on top of her head in a messy bun. Tufts of hair stuck out above her ears like whiskers. "I got a call from a friend. I need to go in the zoo for a bit."

"What's wrong?" I asked. Mom never went into the zoo at night unless there was trouble. Usually *big* trouble, like if one of her animals is sick or hurt.

She shook her head. "I'm afraid there's been an accident," she said. I could tell by the way she avoided my eyes that she was trying not to worry me, but that deep eleven wrinkled between her eyes gave her away. "An animal has been brought in. Hit by a car."

"Oh no! Why are they calling you? Is it going to be okay?" I couldn't stop the string of questions from pouring out. Mom usually worked with the lions at the zoo, so unless it was an actual *lion* that had been hit by a car, why would they need her? And that didn't seem likely, seeing how we don't exactly live in Africa.

"I can catch you up later, hon." She checked her watch anxiously. "I need to get there quickly. Where did I put my jacket?" She started down the hallway, rubbing her temples as she searched.

I bolted back into my bedroom and pulled on some jeans and a sweater. "Hang on," I yipped. "I can come with you! Maybe I can help!" I hated the idea of some poor animal—whatever it was—lying there hurt. Already my throat felt tight, like someone was strangling me with sharp fingers.

Mom had found her jacket and was zipping it up. "It's very late, Ana," she said. "You should go back to bed—you've got school tomorrow." She picked up her keys and headed for the door.

"I'm already dressed! And you *know* there's no way I'll be able to get back to sleep. I can help!" I tried to look as mature as possible, channeling teenagery assertiveness into my voice.

It must have worked because Mom's shoulders slumped. "Fine," she conceded. "Go tell your father you're coming with me and meet me in the car in exactly thirty seconds," she said. "Dress warm and bring a scarf. It's freezing out there."

A few minutes later, Mom and I were zipping away in her truck.

"So you don't know what it is? What got hit, I mean?" I asked, watching the trees fly by us in the white light of our headlights.

Mom was chewing her lip, gripping the steering wheel tightly. "I want you to make sure you stay back, well out of the way, okay? Wild animals can be unpredictable, especially when they're hurt," she said, clearly distracted by her own thoughts. Her eyes swept back and forth, watching the road carefully as we drove. The highway looked eerily creepy this late at night. Like the start of practically every horror film Liv and I would sneakily watch on the Scream Channel when her parents weren't listening.

"I promise," I said, squishing my chin deeper into my scarf. "But what is it?"

She glanced down quickly at the speedometer, drumming her fingers impatiently on the wheel. "A fox," she said. "Someone hit a fox."

Chapter 8

Mallard ducks are known as "dabbling ducks." To eat, they tip upside down in the water with their rumps in the air.

—*Animal Wisdom*

I always thought ducks were cute, but NOW I realize they spend half their time MOONING us when they eat.

When we pulled into the veterinary center at the zoo, I shivered at how dark and empty everything looked. The sporadic swish of flashlights lit up the misty darkness as we parked the car.

"Is it going to be really bad?" I asked as I hopped out of the car. It was sort of surreal to think that the world stayed so busy when I was tucked away asleep in bed. Was every night so exciting?

Mom threw her keys in her pocket and wrapped an arm around me. "I'm not sure, hun. Cars can do a lot of damage."

My mouth went dry. "But why you guys? I mean, aren't there people who do this that don't work at the zoo? Wildlife re…re-*somethings*?" My eyes stung under the fluorescent lights of the clinic as we stepped inside.

"Rehabbers, yes," Mom said, shutting the door tight behind us.

Instantly, I spotted a steel table with something furry and red on it. Most of it was covered by a thick, blue blanket, but I could easily make out two black, furry paws sticking out the back. A fluffy white-tipped tail hung limply off the side of the table.

Chills tingled up my spine.

He was bigger than I'd expected.

"I'm good friends with the wildlife caretaker at the rehab center we're connected with, and she asked if I would help out tonight since she can't be here for an hour. We'll transfer the fox there once he's stabilized," she explained. "I haven't worked with local animals in ages," she said. "But I have to do *something*…" She trailed off.

A swell of pride surged through me as the group

inside the clinic lit up to see Mom walk into the room. It can be easy to forget that Mom was more than the person who made horrible Kraft mac and cheese and washed our socks, but at times like this, when she was stepping up and being awesome and saving wild animals and stuff, it made my heart feel extra big and proud of her.

"Jane." A man with a thick beard and a red flannel shirt reached out to shake her hand. "Thanks for coming so quickly."

Mom smiled. "No problem, Eli," she said. "This is my daughter, Ana. She's going to stay out of the way and watch," she said, for my ears only. I nodded solemnly. I had a feeling this wasn't exactly the time or place to whip out a camera to film everything for my documentary, but holy hedgehogs, I was dying to capture this.

His hand was warm compared to mine. "Nice to meet you, Ana," he said. "You're the spitting image of your mom. Let's get to it?" He approached the table.

"You bet," Mom said.

And instantly, she transformed.

Instead of being my mother, she turned into a machine. But I don't mean a robot machine. I mean a "let's save this animal" machine. She tossed her jacket onto the hanger on the wall with one arm as she turned on the faucet to scrub her hands with the other. Making sure I was several feet away, she lifted the blanket from the fox's face. Instead of her usual lighthearted, goofbally look, her eyes were fierce and focused.

A breath of awe escaped me as I watched the fox's side rise and fall. I'd seen plenty of animals up close, especially living at the zoo. But usually I was separated from them by thick glass and lots of fences, especially if they had fangs. But this? This was something else entirely. Even though it looked completely unconscious, with heavy pants coming from its open mouth, it still felt so *wild*. The thick fur on its back was rusty orange-red, with a white blaze peeking out in between its front legs.

"Foxes are incredibly adaptable." Eli kept me company at the side of the room. "Lots of animals can't survive in populated areas, but foxes don't seem to care. They'll steal food from garbage cans just as soon as they will find their dinner in the wild."

A ripple of excitement rushed through me. I'd known foxes lived around us, especially outside the city and in the mountains. But I never realized how *beautiful* they were, practically stalking through our own backyards with their sharp eyes and fluffy tails.

"Do they get hit by cars a lot?" I asked. My heart blipped with fear as the fox's tail flicked ever so slightly.

He frowned. "They're usually very good about

staying hidden, but with more and more people developing in their natural habitat, we're noticing more incidents. Sometimes they find themselves on our properties, snooping through our garbage or getting cornered by dogs." He frowned.

"Don't worry." He nudged me, winking. "Your pets are safe."

I grinned. "I have a loudmouth parrot," I told him. "I'm pretty sure Darwin would talk so much the fox would *beg* us to take him back." I watched closely as Mom leaned down to inspect each of the fox's black paws. She pressed gingerly on the center of each paw. His sharp claws extended slightly.

"Whoa." I breathed.

Eli grinned with appreciation. "Pretty cool, huh?"

I nodded, my heart racing. Everything was so quiet, but the excited buzz in my head nearly made me bounce on the spot. *This was so cool.*

We watched as Mom moved on to check out the fox's face and neck.

"His pupils are dilated," she said, shining a flashlight at the fox's face. "I think he's got a concussion. Everything else but that leg looks okay. No signs yet of internal bleeding," she said. "Miraculously," she added. Her eyebrows lifted hopefully. "Let's make sure he's still not in any pain, clean out that cut, and stitch him up."

I took a few steps forward, trying to spot the leg she was talking about. A thin trail of blood was seeping slowly onto the steel table, pooling from what looked like a three-inch gash on the fox's forearm. I cringed. It looked so painful. I rubbed my own arms nervously.

"You're going to give him stitches?" I gaped at her. "Yourself?"

Mom wrung her hands and began riffling through the drawers by the sink. "It needs to get done, and Alex, our tech, can help," she said, gesturing to a woman with a dark bob of hair on her left. Alex gave me a small smile. For someone who routinely worked with big zoo animals, she looked remarkably teensy. What did she do when polar bears needed their shots?

"Don't worry, hun," Alex assured me. "He'll be asleep and won't feel a thing. Your mom will be safe too," she added, winking.

I held my breath as I watched them prepare the fox for his stitches. His eyes were covered again with a towel, and a bottle of clear liquid was squirted over its leg. I bit my lip as deep streaks of red ran off with the fluid, onto the towel placed on the floor. It was scary, but more than *anything* I wished I could be working beside her, helping to save this poor animal's life.

Tufts of black fur fell to the floor as Mom used a little electric trimmer to shave the fox's leg around the cut. My heart seemed to clench tighter and tighter. Seeing such a wild animal lying on a table completely knocked out seemed wrong. He should have been out, running through the forest, leaping over rocks, or chasing rabbits. What would it be like to be so free?

I crossed my fingers and wished that he would get better.

"You may not want to watch this part," Mom said, as she set a tray of stitching supplies down. "He's not feeling any pain, but it's not going to be pretty."

"It's okay, Mom," I said. The truth was, despite being totally scary and horrible, it was also seriously *fascinating*, seeing how they did everything and how animals looked up close like this. Before today, I wasn't sure what I wanted to be when I grew up. Maybe a filmmaker like Grandpa?

But now I was wondering if maybe I could be a veterinarian.

Or both?

I imagined myself in green scrubs, bustling around a clinic like this. Saving animals, giving injections, getting to touch such amazing creatures. *Hopefully* not getting my head ripped off.

My fingernails dug into my palm as I watched

Mom and Alex, stitching the raw pink skin of the fox's leg together. What started out looking horrific and dangerous turned into something neat, tidy, and clean.

Bad to good.

Sick to healthy.

Just like that.

When they finally wrapped the final strip of bright-blue dressing around his paw, I relaxed.

"Wow." I breathed. "That was *amazing*." I took another step closer.

Mom grinned, but there was a thin line of sweat that had started beading down her temple. "Do you want to touch him?" she asked. "He's out like a light."

"They feel really cool," Alex said, persuading me. I didn't need much coaxing.

"Heck yes, I do," I said.

I approached the table, feeling a well of heat build up inside of my chest. Even with Mom working with the lions at the zoo, I'd never been able to touch any of them, mainly because they're all adults and would likely tear my face off. And sure, I'd touched crocodiles, but they're so scaly. This was different. This was *wild*.

I leaned closer to the fox's face. His eyes were still half-open in his sleepy daze, and the warm, rusty-orange color looked like it was lined perfectly with black eyeliner. His nose was surrounded by a smattering of wiry, black whiskers.

"He's so beautiful," I said, petting him lightly on the shoulder. His fur was thick and soft, warm against my skin. "Is he going to be okay?"

Alex nodded. "We were lucky they only clipped him with their car. It could have been a lot worse. Now that he's been examined and stitched up, we can take him to the rehabilitation center to heal. Then when they're sure he's okay"—she stroked his paw gently as she talked—"they'll release him."

I sucked in a breath. "He'll be nearby! Mom, can I come and visit him? And can I go with them when he gets released?" I begged.

Beside me, Eli snickered. "Oh, she's your daughter all right," he said.

Mom stretched her arms above her head, then bent down to touch her wriggling fingers to the floor. "I think we can figure all that out when it's not..." She paused, looking at her watch. Her eyes widened. "Two twenty-five in the morning," she said. "You have to be in school soon, kiddo!"

Now, normally when I was stuck heading to school after a long night without sleep, I'd be pretty upset. But this time, I couldn't even pretend. Some nights are worth looking like a zombie the next morning, even though I knew Ashley wouldn't let me hear the end of it about the dark circles under my eyes.

But tonight? It was *definitely* a zombie-worthy night.

On the way home, I couldn't keep the smile from my face. Rolling down the window to feel the cold air on my face, I leaned against the side of my seat.

"What are you so giggly about over there?" Mom asked. It wasn't just me who was feeling extra jazzed—she was now tapping the steering wheel to the beat in her head when she asked.

"What you guys did with that fox," I said. "It was amazing. I think it might be neat to do that…as a job, I mean." I trailed my fingertips out of the window, letting the wind's cold chill start to numb them.

"You want to be a veterinarian?" she asked. Her eyes flicked over to me as she drove. "I think you'd be a great one. It's lots of schooling, but you've definitely got what it takes."

I rolled the window back up, poking my fingers with my other hand as the feeling rushed back to them in hot waves. "I like the idea of taking something so…*broken*," I said. "And fixing it.

You turned that awful gash into something clean, and from there he can heal and live his life again, you know?"

She nodded. "I thought about being a veterinarian in school. My first few years were actually pre-vet."

I tilted my head at her. I didn't know any of this. Why was it so hard to picture parents being *young*, without having kids? It was like opening a book and finding nothing but blank pages. It felt downright *wrong*. I wondered what Mom did for her thirteenth birthday.

"But there is more than one way to help save animals too," she noted. "Your father and I like to think we save them by helping them live happy lives, studying them, and teaching others about them. Your grandfather does the same thing." She grinned cheekily. "Only *he* does it in front of a worldwide audience on the big screen. He always was a drama queen." She clicked her tongue.

"Hey," I ventured. The idea had been sizzling away in my head since I'd met the fox, but now was the first time I'd had a chance to ask. "Do you think that maybe I could help them out?"

Mom blinked, still staring ahead at the road. "Who?"

"At the wildlife rehabilitation place, I mean," I said. "I know the zoo is great, but if the wildlife center will take volunteers…maybe I could go and help out? If it's close, I mean."

Mom's face broke into a wide smile. "I think that's a lovely idea," she said. "I know they're always extremely busy. I can call my friend Kate. She helps run the place. But so you know"—her voice became low—"it won't be like working at the zoo, okay, kiddo? It's very hard work, and messy, and the animals you'll be with won't have any history of being around people. You'll have to be extra, *extra* careful."

"I promise," I said, settling back and snuggling into my jacket. "Thanks!"

As I watched the trees whip by, I thought about what it might be like to be a grown-up and save things that needed saving. It would probably be the coolest feeling ever, getting to save something that, without you, might not have survived.

Then I realized that maybe I didn't need to be a grown-up to save something. There was already a wound in my own life that needed saving, only it wasn't a paw or a tail or even an animal at all.

It was a friendship.

My seat belt tightened as Mom drove faster down the winding highway. Liv and I were like that fox, weren't we? An unhappy accident—her moving far away so many months ago—had changed things in an instant, like a car hitting an animal. And now we were struggling because we didn't know how to be friends anymore, just like that fox was struggling to live.

Mom and her crew had come along to fix him up. But who would fix *us* up?

It had to be me.

Maybe the wildlife rehab place could teach me how.

Chapter 9

The teeth of gray squirrels never stop growing.

—*Animal Wisdom*

I had a dream like this once, where my teeth grew and grew and nothing I did could stop them, so eventually I looked like I was part rodent. I wonder if squirrels have stress dreams?

Sometimes I wonder how grown-ups expect us to stay on top of our lives when there's so much going on.

Like, I bet when my parents were my age, their biggest problem was what to pack for lunch or what outfit to wear at the spring fling. (Or whatever they used to call dances back in the olden days. I have no idea. They were probably filmed in black and white though.)

But to me, it felt like life was full of one problem after another. I couldn't focus on *one* thing. Instead I had to juggle everything, like a seal trying to balance five different plastic balls on my nose.

It was all very stressful.

One ball on my nose was not letting my friendship with Liv get ruined, despite all the weirdness between us. I hoped that including her in my media project would help, but that wasn't going to happen until I actually started to *work* on it.

When I met Sugar at the zoo after school the next day, I was eager to start my very first documentary lesson. I kept picturing myself as a famous wildlife documentary filmmaker, perched at the top of some ancient tree in the middle of the rain forest so I could film some brand-new species they'd name after me.

I wonder if they have awards for "Coolest Filmmaker Named after an Anaconda." Because I would *so* win that.

"Okay, sweet pea!" Sugar trilled. She shivered as she stepped in from the cold, unbuttoning her jacket and pulling her fluffy scarf over her head. "I've got your camera, and I can show you the ropes today to start! I'm so excited to be helping you!"

I hoisted the heavy pack from her shoulders. "So where do we start?" I peered at the camera anxiously. It looked expensive, with all sorts of buttons on the sides. I had expected she would bring one of those giant cameras that Grandpa's camera crew always cart around on their shoulders, but this thing looked teensy in comparison.

Sugar took the camera from its case and handed it to me. "Start with this!" she said. "This is your new best friend, and it will do all the work for you if you let it!"

I slipped my hand through the grip and held it up, pretending like I was focusing on Sugar. It felt pretty fun holding such an expensive gadget, even though I had no idea where the on button was. Of course, I completely forgot about the lens cap. Sugar reached up and clicked it off, handing it to me.

"Throw this in your pocket. I thought we could go around and you could practice using it here, and then I can help you work out any kinks as we go. Sound good? We'll worry about post later on, when you have footage." Her usual bubbly attitude seemed shadowed by her businesslike manner.

"Post?" I asked, lowering the camera.

She nodded. "That's postproduction," she explained. "That's where I'll show you how to edit parts of it together, and even add some music if you like."

The possibilities grew in my head.

Ana Wright: Academy Award–Winning Filmmaker...

Sugar laughed. "If you want to impress your teacher, tell him you're making a *cinema verité*." She drew the words out with a French accent.

"What's that?!" I asked. "It sounds like a pastry. A tasty one too."

My stomach growled.

"It means 'film truth,' but it's a fancy way of saying you're doing a more laid-back type of shooting, with available light, a handheld camera, and all that."

"*Cinema verité*," I repeated. I liked the sound of that. Now I could get an Academy Award *and* wear a cool beret to the award ceremony. I'd probably be besties with Anne Hathaway and Jennifer Lawrence before the night was over.

"You're going to need to know how to turn this thing on first," she said. She reached down and pointed out the buttons I would need. "When this light is red, you're good to go! What do you want to film? We can go anywhere you want!"

I searched around us for a perfect location. "Why don't we start in the Marine Adventure Zone?" I asked. "That might give us some cool underwater footage we could use as an opener-type thing?"

Sugar beamed. "You already sound like a pro. Let's do it!"

If there's anything cooler than seeing sharks and other marine creatures in real life, it's *filming* them so other people can see them from your eyes. Ever since Grandpa had helped fund the aquarium and Marine Adventure Zone during the summer, it had been one of the busiest parts of the zoo. I always loved visiting, but honestly, it was almost *cooler* being able to film it, capturing all the animals forever on video. For once, I could show people exactly what I loved about the place, from my own perspective.

When Sugar and I stepped into the dreamy, blue exhibit, I made sure to hold my camera steady, panning from left to right slowly. I stumbled over my own feet, so there would definitely be some footage I'd have to take out. A powerful feeling of exhilaration swept through me as I realized *everything* I was seeing was being filmed as I walked, trapped forever in my camera.

So much exhilaration, in fact, that I nearly bowled into someone leaning over the tide pool touch tank.

"Ouch! Watch where you're—*Ana*?!"

I fumbled with my camera, trying to turn it off. "Sorry!" I yelped. Ashley was rubbing her forehead with her palm. "Oh! Hey, I didn't know you would be here today."

Ashley shook her head, eyeing the camera. "Some days you get weirder and weirder, Scales," she said.

I rolled my eyes. Ever since Ashley and I had become friends, she'd promised she wouldn't call me Scales anymore. But that didn't stop her from saying it "jokingly."

"What's with the camera?" She poked at it in my hand.

"Have you met Sugar?" I asked, waving Sugar over from her favorite tank of moon jellies.

Ashley's eyes nearly popped out of her head as Sugar scuttled over and shoved out her hand. "Pleased to meet you!" Sugar said. "I'm Sugar! Ana's grandfather's girlfriend," she added quickly.

"Oh!" Ashley squeaked. "You're like, super gorgeous! You know that, right? Wow…"

I rolled my eyes as Ashley gawked.

"What she means is, *hello*." I shoved Ashley. To be honest, it was pretty great to introduce Ashley to Sugar, because I knew Sugar was *exactly* what Ashley wanted to be like when she was older. Picture perfect with the world's greatest shoes.

Ashley blushed hot pink. "Sorry…"—she stammered—"I've heard a lot about you." She flipped her hair back coolly. "It's great to meet you finally."

Sugar nodded. "Pleasure's all mine, sweetheart! I'll give you guys a moment. I want to get a picture of these adorable jellies; I have to every single time I'm in here! Then we can keep going through some exhibits for you, Ana!" She scurried away, leaving Ashley awestruck.

"Those *shoes*," she said, leaning in close to whisper. "I'd seen her around with your Grandpa before, but I've never seen her up close. She's seriously gorge, right?"

I nodded. "She is. She's also super nice, and she knows a ton about cameras and filming too." I grinned as I watched Sugar center her camera phone to snap a photo of the jellies. "I like having her around. She's helping me with that media project at school."

"So that's what you're doing with the gadget, huh?" Ashley pointed to my camera as she sat down on the ledge beside the touch tank. She was in her blue volunteer shirt, but the gold hoops in her earlobes made her almost look dressy.

"You got it," I said proudly. "I'm doing a documentary, and Sugar lent me some equipment." I gripped the camera tightly in my hand. I didn't mention that my documentary would *also* help me get things back to normal with Liv, which was way more important than any school credit.

Ashley's eyes widened. "Ooh, that's a great idea. I wish I'd thought of that. I'm doing a blog post where I'm going to embed songs for each person I'm talking about. Mr. Nicholson said that I'll need to include an explanation of why I picked each song though." She scrunched up her nose.

"That's a cool idea," I said. *Not as cool as a real documentary though*, I thought gleefully. "Who are you going to talk about?"

She shrugged. "Probably some friends," she said. "You'll be on the list though, so if you have any song requests, let me know."

"Me?" I asked, nearly dropping my camera. I swung the strap over my shoulder to avoid any accidents involving the shark tank.

Ashley shrugged. "Why not? You're the reason I'm *here*, aren't you? I'll have to think of the world's geekiest song though." She dipped her hand below the surface of the water to skim the top of a passing epaulette shark.

"Aw, thanks," I said. "Hey, what about Rayna?" I asked suddenly. "You and her were always hanging out together last year. What happened there?" The truth was, I *knew* that Rayna and Ashley had stopped hanging out at the beginning of the school year, and since hanging out with *me* was the only thing that had changed in Ashley's life, I couldn't help but think I'd had something to do with their friendship fizzling. As much as I didn't like Rayna, the thought that something so small could ruin a friendship made my chest tight.

Ashley shrugged. "You know the drill." She bent her fingers, inspecting her nails. "I mean, we hung out a lot the past couple years, but you *know* she's been a total pill since school started."

Now, to *me*, that didn't sound any different than normal old Rayna. She had been Ashley's friend back when Ashley was a mean Sneerer, so I always assumed when Ashley started acting nicer toward me, her friends Rayna and Brooke would do the same. Brooke and I get along, but Rayna stayed as mean as ever. And Rayna seemed to get more distant from Ashley until I rarely saw them together.

"But you guys were best friends," I pointed out. "That should matter, right? *Best* friends can't suddenly not talk to each other or not be friends at all." I hated that I could hear the uncertainty in my own voice, like I was waiting or hoping for Ashley to correct me.

But she didn't.

Instead, she shook her head. "I don't know." She sighed. "Like, think about it." She pointed to me. "*You* used to be my enemy, you know? And now you're not. If that can change, then who's to say that best friends can't suddenly become…*not* friends?"

I shook my head, feeling my cheeks get hot. "But it's not the same thing! Friends can't just—"

"I think they can, Ana!" Ashley interrupted. Her eyes were glassy. She turned away to let her hand drag in the water again, skimming against the current. "People can change," she said. "Doesn't matter if they're your friend or not. You grow up or grow apart or whatever."

I gripped my camera tighter, searching for the perfect explanation to show she was wrong. My doubts about Liv and I felt like they were cuts on my skin, getting more exposed every day.

"So," Ashley said, her lip drawing up slightly. "I hear Liv's back for a visit."

I sucked in a breath. Could she read my mind? "Um, yeah."

"Does she know we're friends now?" she asked. She twirled her hair as her ears turned pink again. "I mean, does she know that we aren't like…"

At each other's throats?

I nodded. "She knows," I lied quickly. "It's totally fine. She's here for a couple weeks. She's spent the last few days visiting her relatives a few hours away. And she has purple hair now," I babbled. I had a feeling that even if you told a lie, it was possible to bury it with enough truths so people wouldn't notice. Like throwing a pile of clean socks on a single dirty one.

"That's cool," she said.

I was super lucky that Ashley didn't know my lie face as well as Liv did. Before she could ask anything else, Sugar returned. She showed us the pictures she'd taken on her phone as her eyes danced with excitement.

"Oh, I *do* love it here! Are you ready to do some practice runs with the camera? We can get some footage at the Croc Pavilion if you like!"

Waving good-bye to Ashley, Sugar started coaching me through how to set up certain shots for my documentary. I listened to every word, and even took notes in my journal so I could use every trick I could to make this the greatest documentary anyone—especially Liv—had ever seen. I couldn't let what happened to Rayna and Ashley happen to us. We *couldn't* grow apart.

Possible Titles for My Documentary, Now That I've Mastered the Art of Turning the Camera On and Taking the Lens Cap Off:

1. *My Life: An Award-Winning Documentary* (I like this one, but it might sound a *bit* too ambitious.)
2. *The Eighth-Grade Life of Ana Wright* (This one sounds like a made-for-TV movie where someone dies at the end. No thanks.)

3. *How to Lie to One Friend about Being Friends with Another Friend: No, Seriously, It's Okay Because Soon Everything Will Be Sorted Out and Nobody Will Mind That You Waited to Tell the Truth to Liv and Ashley Because You Didn't Want Either of Them to Get Upset* (Too confusing. Darn it.)

Chapter 10

Great horned owls are one of the few animals that regularly eat skunks. Sometimes
they eat them so often, even their nests and
feathers may smell musky.

—Animal Wisdom

Eww! There would be nothing worse than spending your life reeking of skunk! Maybe that's
why Daz's room smells so much like Cheetos?
That's practically all he eats.

"So what is it you want me to do again?" Daz sat
taller on the couch. Darwin was sitting beside him
on the cushion, and they were both preening. At
least I knew that Darwin didn't have fleas; I couldn't

say the same for Daz. Beside him, Kevin sat with a notepad sprawled over his lap. Like me, Kev loved to doodle, but he didn't doodle animals and stuff like I did. Instead, he drew robots and super-serious blueprints for an artificial intelligence that may take over humankind at any moment.

You know, genius stuff.

"*You* wanted to do this, not me!" I reminded him. Ever since Daz heard about my documentary plans, he was practically frothing at the mouth for me to include him in it. He even promised to say what I told him to say and not embarrass me in *any* way possible.

Fat chance of that, right?

I peeked at the camera again to check Daz's position through the viewfinder. It was hard to not train the camera on Kevin, looking all adorable as he sat there trying to stay out of Daz's way. Good thing I was a professional.

"I can't *not* be in your documentary," he said, rolling his eyes. "It's supposed to be about people who made you who you are today, right? Tell me that I haven't done that. *Tell me* that Ana Wright would even exist without this." His gestured to himself proudly. One of Darwin's feathers was stuck in his hair, but I didn't mention it. I remembered what Sugar said about capturing people realistically, without any extra effort to make them look a certain way.

Plus, it was funny to see Daz covered in bird fluff.

"I'm only talking about five things, and sorry, my skeezy brother does not rank high on my influence list. No offense. Be thankful you're in it at all!" I yanked open the curtain, letting the last of the late-afternoon light into the room like Sugar had taught me. Darwin fluttered his wings in the warmth.

Daz beamed. "Okay, I'm ready. Ten four. Roger dodger. Let's do this thing." He finger-gunned me and winked.

"Ew, don't do that on camera, okay? It's seriously creepy," I said. Getting behind the camera, I carefully hit the record button and started to count down, exactly the way Sugar had taught me.

Kevin piped up. "Totally creepy," he said. But Daz sent a pillow sailing for his face.

"Five, four, three…" I continued with my fingers and pointed for Daz to start.

Immediately he launched into his speech, with the prompt cards I'd given him still stuck under him on the seat. "Hello, and welcome to Ana Wright's official documentary, all about how she manages to spend so much time in the bathroom, and yet still somehow looks the same when she comes out."

"*Cut!*" I shouted. Daz cackled with laughter as I stormed over to the couch and yanked the cards out from under him. "These." I shoved them into his hands. "You are supposed to use *these*. You're introducing my documentary, and telling people that I am going to be talking about who influences me and showing the world how they helped make me who I am today." I gave him my very dirtiest glare, throwing as much sincere "do not mess with me now" anger behind it.

Obviously it wasn't glarey enough because Daz cracked up again. "Okay, okay!" he said. "I was trying out some improv. You're getting pretty moody in your old age, huh?"

"Don't remind me," I said, marching back behind the camera.

"*Brack! Old age banana!*" Darwin crowed, enjoying Daz's high-pitched antics. I glared at him too.

"Oh, come on." He leaned back on the couch, nearly knocking Darwin from his cushion. "Hey, we should tell Mom what we want for a party! We can't have something lame for thirteen." He tilted his head back and yelled. "Hey! Ma!"

"Daz!" I fumed. "This isn't the time for parties. You're supposed to be helping me with my project, and I didn't even *want* your help in the first place, but you told me that you'd stick my toothbrush in Dwayne 'The Rock' Johnson's cage if I didn't."

Honestly. Brothers cannot be human. Right when you think they're getting more normal and being somewhat nicer to you, they go and get all… *brothery* on you all over again.

"Fine, geez," he said, straightening up again. He ran his fingers through his hair, ensuring it was extra spiky. "This is Daz Wright, and I'm here today to introduce Ana's Wright's official documentary. In it, we will learn that—"

"Stop!" I shouted.

Daz froze with his mouth still open. The card in his hand trembled as he struggled not to move. "What is it this time?"

I pointed to the camera. "You didn't let me say go! It wasn't even running."

"But it was perfect!" he whined.

"So do it again!" I counted down behind the camera and hit record.

He sighed, launching back into his monologue. "This is Daz Wright, and I'm—"

"Did someone call me?" Mom yelled down from the top of the staircase.

"*Dazmanian devil!*" Darwin shrieked.

"Oh, for the love of Pete!" I turned the camera off and collapsed onto the floor. Did all filmmakers have such a hard time with their subjects? I couldn't imagine any of Grandpa's filmmakers struggling to get footage like this. Wild bonobos were probably easier to wrangle than my idiot brother and my loudmouthed, diva parrot.

"Yeah!" Daz called, waving Mom over. He climbed up onto the back of the couch and bounced on his butt. "We want to talk birthdays!"

I rolled over and tucked my camera out of the way before Daz bulldozed over it by accident.

"What's this?" Mom slinked down the stairs, trying to hide her smile. She was carrying a hardcover textbook with wild cats on the cover, and she was still in her work shirt, even though she'd changed into a pair of holey, faded jeans. "Are there two important birthdays coming up in this household? Whoever could they be?" She crossed her arms and drummed her fingertips.

I couldn't help but smile at how chill she looked in the face of Daz's bounciness. Mothers must be immune to their own kids' brand of crazy, I swear.

"It's thirteen, Mom," I said, joining in. Grandpa always says if you can't beat 'em, join 'em, but really I was excited at the possibility of cake. "We should do something fun for thirteen, don't you think?"

Mom eyed Daz. "Maybe we can talk after you stop treating our poor couch like a combat zone," she said. He sighed dramatically and slid his butt down back to the cushion. I tsked at him, trying to get Mom on my side now so she'd side with me on the birthday party ideas.

"It so happens that your father and I have discussed the possibility for a party for our dear baby twins." She scrunched her nose at us playfully. "What did you guys have in mind?"

Daz leaped up. "Laser tag party!" he squealed. "Dinosaur party! Dinosaurs *with* lasers party!"

Kevin lit up. "Ooh, that's a good one!"

Honestly.

Mom shook her head. "So mature for his age."

I don't know if it's a weird-brother thing or not, but dinosaurs and lasers was *not* my idea of a cool teenager party. It sounded more like a party for eight-year-olds. I was only going to turn thirteen once. Did I seriously want to do it while running for my life from Daz while he shot lasers at me?

Pretty sure I would have the rest of my life to deal with that.

"Maybe we could have something at the zoo?" I asked. It seemed only fitting. When I turned twelve, I had no idea how much the zoo would play a role in my life. Now it felt like a second home, where so many important things had happened. I'd started doing public presentations there, and even Daz had loved living there. It could be the perfect spot for a supercool teenager party, especially since so many people didn't get to visit as often as I did. *Ooh*, and I could film some of it for my documentary!

Daz pointed at me. "I like it. We could take over the whole zoo! With lasers!" He started rapping, spraying beads of spittle all over himself. "Ain't no party like a dino party, 'cause a dino party's got lasers!"

"Let's back that trolley up, young man," Mom said, gesturing for him to shush. "We can't take over the whole zoo, but I see no reason why we can't use the banquet hall behind the visitor's center for a nice little party. It would make things so much simpler if we did a party for the two of you together. You're both okay with that, right?"

I rolled my eyes. "Sure, make me share my special day with him," I pretend-whined. As long as we weren't expected to share a cake, I'd pretty much accepted every birthday of mine was going to be Dazzified, being twins and all.

"Whatever, loser. It's *my* special day too! The day I become a *man*!" He reached for a pillow to throw at me, startling Darwin away.

Good Lord.

"It's a special day for *both* of you," Mom said. Her lip quivered as she looked at the two of us for a beat too long. "My babies, turning thirteen."

I scrambled from the floor, swinging Darwin up onto my shoulder. Daz, being an android and therefore totally unable to read human emotion, nodded proudly.

"That's right! The big one three. I should start looking into retirement plans. Do I need to make a will? I don't want all my robots getting into the wrong hands if I die," he said, scratching his chin.

"It's okay, Mom," I said, patting her awkwardly on the back. "It's not that old," I lied.

I mean, we all *knew* that thirteen was pretty much *the* biggest birthday milestone one can have, right? But I wasn't about to say that to Mom having a melt-down. Besides, it sort of freaked me out too. But if anything would make me feel less terrified about it, it was a birthday party in a place that I knew I loved.

"The banquet thing would be perfect," I said. "We can invite everyone and have some fun games and—"

"And *lasers*!" Daz glared at me pointedly.

"Shoot," Kevin said suddenly, checking his watch. He stood up and folded his notebook closed, stuffing it into his backpack. He eyed me apologetically. "Sorry, I have to head out. We're supposed to video chat with my brother tonight to make sure everything's okay for next week." He turned to Mom. "We're going away for a few days to visit him," he explained, heading for the door.

"Have a good visit, hun," she said. "I'll miss

having you around to make sure Daz doesn't burn anything down." She rolled her eyes.

He grinned, then looked to me. "I'll…uh…see you later?"

I shifted a few feet closer to the front door. In case you were wondering, the "official good-bye" with your kind-of boyfriend in front of your brother and mother is *the* most awkward thing on the planet.

Worse than when you go to high-five someone and end up missing their hand like a lame-o, even.

Do you kiss? Do you *not* kiss? Do you hug? The whole thing was a disaster waiting to happen.

"'Kay," I said, stepping closer. He went in for a quick hug, while I accidentally dodged the wrong way and ended up colliding with his shoulder.

Smooth, Ana.

"See you at later," I added, practically feeling Mom's giggly stare behind me. *This* was why people need to forget the whole "first kiss" thing, because at this rate, it definitely *wasn't* going to happen for me.

"Well, that was gross," Daz said plainly after Kevin left.

"Hey!" I shouted. "I have to watch you and Bella stare at each other all googly-eyed!" I stuck out my chin. It occurred to me right then that my *brother* might get his first kiss before me. Oh, *GAH*.

Daz scoffed. "Whatever! It's not the same thi—"

"*Anyway*," Mom said, breaking us up. "I think a zoo party sounds like a great plan. I'm on it!"

"Hey," I said, thinking back on all my earlier birthdays. Now that Kevin was gone, my brain seemed to be able to function again. (Figures.) "Do you think I could have a slumber party after?" Ever since we became best friends, Liv and I had special birthday sleepovers every year. Usually we made lip gloss and talked about boys and all the things we wanted to happen during the next year of our lives. Maybe that was exactly what we needed right now.

Mom nodded. "I think that's a great idea. You girls will have to stay in the basement though. Four is too many for upstairs. Daz would never leave you alone either," she muttered.

"Oh," I said, realizing what she meant. "I don't mean with everyone, just Liv and me. Like old times."

"No Bella or Ashley?" she asked. Her head tilted with concern, but I didn't want her to worry.

"I think since Liv is back, it would be nice to have her over," I said. "You know, she's only here for a little while, and I can have a sleepover with Bella or Ashley anytime."

It's true I would feel bad not inviting Bella or Ashley, but I had to do everything I could to keep Liv and I together as best friends, didn't I? After all, she wasn't around here for long, so Bella and Ashley would both probably understand. I could have them over anytime after she went home again.

Mom pursed her lips, considering this. "Okay, if that's what you want. Make sure not to leave anyone out at the party."

I nodded, but already the thought of having Liv and Ashley in the same room together was making my stomach twist up like a pretzel. *That* was definitely something I'd have to figure out later, without Mom staring at me.

"If Ana gets to have Liv over, can Kevin stay too?" Daz piped in. "It's only fair!"

I gulped. If there was one thing that I *wasn't* ready for about being thirteen was the possibility of having Kevin stay over at our place during sleepovers with Daz. Sure, he'd stayed here a zillion times before, but that was *before* all the hand-holding and stuff. What if he saw me in my nightshirt or something? Or worse, walking around in one of those green face masks that Ashley was always hounding me to try?

The potential for embarrassment was way too high.

"How about you stay over at his place?" Mom said, eyeing me. I shifted uncomfortably.

I could tell by the look on his face that Daz had no idea what awkward thoughts were going through my head. But judging by the hard determination in Mom's eyes, she had completely read my mind.

Talk about terrifying.

"Deal," Daz said.

"Excellent!" Mom announced, pulling her ponytail tighter. "I'll let your father know we'll be setting it up at the zoo, and what you guys can do to help us out is make a list of everyone you want invited, all right? I'll also make sure Dad and Sugar know. I'm sure they'll want to join us." She pulled out the notepad in her jeans pocket and scribbled a message. "I can't believe my babies are thirteen," she added wistfully.

I stepped back, causing Darwin to hop over to Mom's shoulder in protest. "Hey! I'm not thirteen yet. I've got a few more days," I pointed out. I could practically hear the ticking clock in my head, counting down the last hours of my twelve-year-old self.

"Enjoy them," Mom said, her eyes crinkling. "And by the way! I called Kate at the Safe Haven Wildlife Center, and you're on for your first volunteer session tomorrow! Dad can drop you off, but make sure you bring the immunization card I left on your bed, okay? And you should also bring a change of coveralls, so you don't drag home God knows what afterward, okay?"

I gasped. "I totally forgot about the wildlife center!" I shrieked, turning to dash up the stairs. "I need to find something to wear!"

Three Things That Suck about Sharing a Birthday with a Boy (Specifically, Your Brother)

1. No matter what you do, he will always try to blow out all the candles. *Even* if you have two cakes, and only one of them is for him. That means gross boy spit all over your icing.
2. For the rest of your life, you will have to endure extra-loud-in-your-ear singing when everyone sings "Happy Birthday" to you because he knows you hate that song.
3. You'll have to hear endlessly about how you're an "old geezer," simply because you happen to be born *four minutes* before him.

Chapter 11

A bison's hump is made of muscle, which allows it to push its way through snow with its head like a snowplow.

—*Animal Wisdom*

This would come in handy on those snowy January mornings when we're late for school, but it would be impossible to find a coat to fit over it, wouldn't it? I'd probably look like that Quasimodo guy, who lived in the castle. Or was it a clock tower?

I'm fine.

I'm fine. I am calm, cool, collected, and supersmart. I'm almost thirteen years old, and I can handle whatever happens today.

The minute Dad dropped me off at the Safe Haven Wildlife Center, I couldn't wait to get started. I could help rescue wolves! And release bald eagles! And ride moose!

Okay, so I definitely knew that riding moose was out of the question, but that didn't stop me from imagining myself on the summit of some mountain with an eagle on my shoulder. Maybe I should have worn a Katniss braid?

I tugged my ponytail tighter and stuffed my gloves into my pocket before glancing up at the door to the main clinic. Mom told me that the center was designed with the animals in mind, with several buildings and cages in groups that were well away from human activity. Unlike the zoo, human eyes were the *last* thing these animals needed, because the more people they interacted with, the more likely they would approach them in the wild. That would be bad news.

The biggest building—the clinic with two huge windows at the front—was where I was told to check in.

"Deep breath," I told myself, turning the knob and stepping through. "Hello?" The reception area was small and empty, so I took another few steps into what looked to be where they checked animals after people dropped them off.

The walls were buttery yellow, and cages, tanks, and aquariums lined every surface. Brightly colored posters of native wildlife lined the walls, along with anatomy posters of several animals, like turtles, birds, and foxes. Cabinets, drawers, and shelves were well labeled, with tiny tags marking their contents, like gauze, syringes, and bandages. A fridge hummed in the corner of the room with a magnet that read "It's Raining Cats and Dogs! I Hope It Doesn't Reindeer!"

I giggled. Clearly these were my people.

I jolted as something stirred in one of the cages, like a crinkling paper sound. Peering over the top of the cage, I braced myself for the worst. I knew these animals were here because they were injured, so I had to expect it, right?

But I couldn't prepare myself for what I saw.

Nope, it wasn't gross or scary.

Instead, it was so ridiculously *cute*.

A tiny squirrel was curled up inside a bunch of shredded newspaper, his nose twitching as I leaned closer. A blue bandage—like the one Mom had given the fox—was wrapped around his front leg.

"Hey, little guy," I whispered. He looked so pitifully adorable. "Do you know where everyone is?"

Just then, the door burst open. A kid with a wool hat and the world's largest rubber boots clattered inside. In his hands was a jet-black bird that glared at me accusingly.

"Who are you?!" he demanded. His jaw was jutted forward, and he seemed to have forgotten he was holding a bird.

"I'm Ana," I said hesitantly. Then I forced myself to stand a little taller. There was no way I was going to let a kid like this freak me out. I'd faced off against crocodiles, *thankyouverymuch*. "I'm a new volunteer here. Today's my first day. Who are you?"

He stomped over to one of the birdcages and tucked the black bird inside, latching the door carefully. "You're not supposed to be in here!" he said, his voice getting higher with each word. "It's against the rules. You're supposed to wait out there," he said matter-of-factly, pointing at the reception area.

"Hey, listen," I said, holding up my hands in apology. "I was looking for Kate?"

"That's enough, Andrew," a sharp Australian voice made us both jump.

I whirled around, facing a woman with short, silvery-gray hair, rosy cheeks, and the dirtiest coveralls I'd ever seen. Spatters of blood, dried milk, and some unidentified brown goo were everywhere.

Though I had a feeling I knew what it was.

"Hi!" I said, determined to make a good first impression. "You must be Kate!" I went to stick out my hand for her to shake it, then noticed she already had a mitt full of—what *were* those?

I took a step back as I realized whatever they were looked very *dead*.

She grinned. "Frozen mousicles for our great horned owl," she explained, dumping the lot of them into a Tupperware on the counter. They clattered like ice cubes. Wiping her palm on her coveralls, she stuck out her hand. "I am indeed Kate, and you must be Ana."

Gulping, I shook her hand, trying to remember Dad's instructions to keep my handshake firm, but not so tight that people would think I was a crazy person. But what do you do when the person whose hand you're shaking was just holding a bunch of dead, frozen mice?

"I am," I said. "Thank you very much for letting me help out today." I smiled, my eyes drifting over to the mice again.

"Say hello, Andrew," Kate instructed, giving me the teensiest wink.

Beside us, Andrew scuffed his boots. "Hello," he said dully.

"At eight years old," Kate said, "Andrew is our youngest volunteer." Her eyebrow quirked. "He's excellent at helping with the birds, and I must say he gets rather *protective* over them." Immediately,

133

with the frozen mice and quirky attitude, I knew I liked her.

"It so happens you came at the perfect time," she said, clapping her hands together. "One of our volunteers couldn't show up today, so I can use the extra hand. Did your bring your immunization record so I can make a copy?" She dug into her pocket as she spoke and pulled out a few almonds, flicking bits of pocket lint from them with her finger. "Care for one?" she asked.

"No thanks," I said. "And yeah, it's right here. Mom made a copy for you to save time."

"What's that for?" Andrew boosted himself up on his tiptoes to see.

"This is to show that Ana here has received all the necessary vaccinations to work with the animals we have here," she explained slowly and carefully for him. At that moment, I was super jealous of her cool Aussie accent. I was pretty sure if I had an accent, people would take me a lot more seriously.

"Is it so she doesn't get rabies?" Andrew asked, eyes wide.

"Precisely." She nodded. She reached up to tap my head with one solid knock. "Can't have your brain swelling up like a unpopped kernel of corn, can we?! Not on your first day! And now we need to make sure someone *else* doesn't get it."

I watched as she rummaged through a drawer and pulled out a small syringe, along with a tiny, wrapped blue needle. "Syringe." She held it up to me. Then she cracked open the package, exposing the blue cap where it would connect with the plastic syringe. "Needle," she said.

I nodded.

"Would you mind going into the fridge and getting me the bottle marked RaVac3, please?"

I blinked, then realized she was talking to me. "Yes, ma'am," I said, scrambling over to the fridge. Thankfully, the key to the lock was still stuck inside. Searching along the door, I found the bottle and handed it to her. Even though I *technically* had no idea what I was doing, I couldn't help but feel a thrill at helping her. That needle was no joke!

"Observe," she instructed. "You want the same amount of air in the syringe that you need for the vaccine before you stick it in the bottle." She pulled the syringe back a teensy bit, then carefully jabbed it into the plastic top of the bottle, tipping the whole thing upside down.

"Then you push the plunger down once inside and pull up however much dose you need."

I swallowed hard. "Will…will I be expected to do this?" My cheeks burned. "I mean, should I take notes or something?"

She eyed me and pulled the needle from the bottle. "Not today you won't have to," she said, smiling. The wrinkles around her eye crinkled even more. "But someday! And you might find that eventually you don't need notes at all! Trust your brain. It's big enough!"

"Right," I said, breathing a little easier. "Gotcha."

"Next, you cap the needle *immediately*," she said, clicking the blue cap into place again. "No excuses. No distractions. No maybes. Immediately!"

"Immediately!" Andrew echoed, giving me a super-serious old-man glare. I was beginning to think this kid was a human version of Darwin, my parrot.

"Got it," I said, taking the bottle from her and putting it back into the fridge. "Now what?"

She grinned widely and turned, starting to march out of the room. Her hand lifted in a victory charge. "Now we go find the wee beastie! Andrew, you're on bird duty while we're busy. Make sure Rupert gets extra mealworms today and do *not* open the Cooper's hawk cage because he *will* bite you! I don't have time to bandage your hand again, you hear me? Ana, grab one of those big garbage bags on the way out and the goggles hanging by the door, please!"

"Yes, ma'am!" He saluted her as I charged out the door, following Kate. For a woman who was clearly in her sixties or seventies, she seemed as spry as Grandpa. I panted after her outside, stuffing the garbage bag into my coveralls as I walked. In the cold air, I was thankful Mom had forced me to wear a pair of long johns, even though they were completely embarrassing and gave me a wedgie. From the look of Kate, she wasn't about to bad-mouth my fashion choices. It was actually sort of *nice* not to think about how I looked, unlike in school where I felt like we were all walking some pretend runway with judges scoring us behind our backs.

"So what kind of animal are we vaccinating?" I asked, falling into step with her. Our rubber boots clomped along in unison on the dirt road away from the clinic.

Her lips formed a thin line. "Some of the volunteers have been calling him Calvin," she said, digging into her pockets and handed me a thick, rubbery pair of gloves. "As in Calvin Klein. But you will know him as the western spotted skunk."

Gulp.

I hunched as low as I could in the cage, trying to keep my head from knocking into the chicken wire that lined the top. The cold air was making my nose run, and the outdoor cages surrounding us looked particularly creepy against the gray sky.

But it was still so *cool*.

So far, Kate and I had not only stepped *willingly* inside a skunk's cage, but now we were supposed to actually catch him, so she could stick him with a needle to make sure he didn't get rabies.

Oh, and to top it off, I was wearing a garbage bag. Apparently the latest technology we have against getting sprayed by skunks was Glad bags and goggles.

Seriously.

I took a deep breath, willing myself to stay relaxed. This definitely wasn't the same as the zoo, but there was something thrilling about the sheer *wildness* of it all. The animals here weren't used to people, and that made them seem even more mysterious. It was a whole different kind of fun.

"The trick to skunks," she said in a whisper. "Is that they give you plenty of warning before they spray. They stomp. They lift their wee rumps in the air. If we are quick enough, you can grab him, tuck his tail, and Bob's your uncle, we'll have it done." She dug into her pocket and popped another almond into her mouth. Her eyes lifted to the darkening sky.

"Tuck his tail?" I asked, my voice squeaking. This plan didn't seem—what was the word again?—*sane*. And who the heck was Bob?

I tried to keep my panic from showing. So far we hadn't spotted the skunk (no pun intended), but from what Kate had told me, he was only a few feet away beneath a pile of logs and dirt.

"Calvin is still very young, one of this year's late fall litters. If you tuck his tail under him in your hands, he won't spray you."

I blinked. It sounded too good to be true. "For real? That's pretty amazing," I said. "Sort of like an off button!"

She nodded. "Kind of. But don't worry, if you don't manage it, it won't be so bad because he's only a wee thing. Go ahead and start slowly digging through those logs. Gloves on, he won't be able to hurt you."

"He won't bite me?" I asked, feeling the dread grow in my stomach. From what *I* knew about animals, anything with sharp teeth *could* and *would* bite you.

"Oh, he'll bite you." She grinned. "But the gloves will keep you safe. Just remember: once you find him, cup your hands around him and get that tail tucked. He's only about the size of your two palms together."

"Okay," I said, psyching myself up. "I'll get him."

I'll get the skunk. I'll get him. I'll go headfirst into a skunk den and stick my hands in there. Sure. No problem.

Gritting my teeth, I gingerly shimmied forward

a few feet and began lifting the logs. Despite the whole "he won't be too stinky" thing, I was already having doubts, because the whole area reeked of skunk. I tucked my goggles up closer on my nose and started breathing through my mouth.

"Heeeere, Calvin," I whispered under my breath. My eyes were glued to the dirt as I shifted the logs, waiting for the telltale black-and-white fur.

And then, I saw it.

"Yesssss!" I hissed, reaching forward as fast as I could. There he was!

Kate was right. He was a teensy little thing, with a fluffy black-and-white-spotted body, tiny little paws, and the cutest face ever. "I got you!"

Wrapping my fingers around him, he immediately started to struggle, but I was too quick. Practically bursting with excitement, I secured his tail with my pinkie finger snugly up against his rump, curling his tail up over his tummy. He hadn't sprayed! I did it! He jerked his head around to bite me, but all he got was a mouthful of rubber glove. His tiny teeth were sharp, but they didn't feel any worse than a bite from Darwin through gloves.

I could do this!

"Fast hands, Ana!" Kate said, clearly impressed. She waved me over closer with the syringe. "Hold him steady now."

I held my breath as Kate injected him with the vaccine and capped the needle again. Pride swam through me like a giddy, leaping dolphin. Because of *me*, this little guy wouldn't get rabies. He had a real chance of surviving out in the wild!

"Excellent work," Kate said, crawling backward out of the cage.

"Thanks!" I said. I took a minute to peer closer at Calvin, at his beady black eyes and the tiny, white claws that gripped the glove so tightly. Now that he was done struggling, he almost seemed to be enjoying himself. "He's so cute, huh?"

She nodded. "They are. All you need to do now is set him down gently and hightail it out of there."

I shuffled back, so I would be closer to the door of the cage when I set him down. Even though it was only my first day, I was already picturing all the things I would get to do here—vaccinating animals like Calvin, helping birds learn to fly, maybe even getting to hang out with bigger stuff like my fox who was somewhere around here—

"Ana, *look out!*"

I blinked, but it was too late.

In my little daydream, my pinkie finger had slipped. Calvin's tail, which *should* have been neatly tucked against him, was stuck straight out from his body like a flag.

A warning flag.

"No!" I struggled to regain where my hands had been, to somehow wrangle him a little tighter to slip my hand under that tail again, but it was useless. He was squirming and scratching again, obviously well aware that I'd messed up and now *he* was the one running the show.

Then it happened.

Skunk spray shot all *over* me.

My goggles.

My garbage bag.

My hands.

My face.

My coveralls.

"*Gah!*" I spat, letting him go to scurry away back to his burrow. The smell—*no*, the taste, like burned onions and pepper—was too much to bear. "He got me! He got me!" I bolted from the cage, getting out of the way while Kate locked it quickly. My coughing echoed through the woods around us.

"So…" she said calmly when I was done hacking. Her own eyes were watering, but she didn't seem to notice that we'd gone from crisp air to biohazard in less than a second.

I stared at her with watery, gloopy eyes. The spit in my mouth still tasted like skunk, and I was pretty sure I would never smell normal again. I would smell like skunk on my *wedding day* if Calvin had any say on the matter.

Kate grinned, her eyes twinkling. "Still think he's cute?"

Chapter 12

Only female mosquitoes can bite humans and other animals. Males eat flower nectar.

—Animal Wisdom

You know, I get that I'm only twelve and three hundred and sixty-three days old (booya, birthday tomorrow!) but I don't get this! Boy mosquitoes get to go around LITERALLY smelling the flowers, while girls have to go out and do all the hard work? And drink blood?! Whatever happened to equality?

How to Survive a Skunk Attack: Ana's Official DeSkunk Plan

(Which, by the way, is probably going to be the name of

my autobiography when I'm an old geezer, because oh my God, this smell is never going to go away, is it?)

1. Forget the tomato sauce. According to Kate, my new friend and skunky-smelling pal, tomatoes do nothing but add an "Italian twist" to your already smelly problem. This is good because it means no disgusting tomato baths. This is bad because, duh, you still reek and you have to walk around with the nickname "Stinkpot."

2. Invest in some of that orange-smelling floor cleaner. Apparently this is the only thing that will give you any hope of a normal life ever again. It won't take the skunk smell away, but it will mask it enough that you can (hopefully) be in the same room as people without making anyone barf. (Always a plus, right?)

3. Wash your hair. Then wash it again. Then wash it again. Then when you're tired of washing it again, WASH. IT. AGAIN.

It's a truth universally acknowledged that a girl who's been sprayed by a skunk named Calvin will also get a horrible grade on her Shakespeare test.

Okay. So I don't actually know that's true, but

it's exactly what happened to me the next day at school. I knew something was up because Mr. Nicholson gave me a weird half smile before the bell rang to dismiss us. Then I *really* knew when he handed out the tests and mine was facedown, with a big fat F on it, along with a red "See me please."

Ugh.

Was anything worse than the "See me please"? You know they're trying to be nice and understanding, but deep down you already feel like you want to climb in a hole because you botched up a test and disappointed them. Teachers should write "Need ice cream?" instead.

When class finished, I tried to make myself look busy, stuffing my notebook into my backpack. I didn't exactly want Ashley or Bella to know why I had to linger behind. I'd seen their tests from my desk, and they'd booth gotten smiley face stickers, so I knew they'd done well.

Staring at my feet with my test rolled up in my hands, I shuffled to the front of the room after everyone had left. Mr. Nicholson was organizing papers on his desk.

"Ana!" he said, looking up. "Thanks for staying for a few minutes." He gestured for me to take a seat.

"You said you wanted to see me," I mumbled. My

test felt like it weighed as much as an elephant in my hands. This was *torture*. "I mean, on my test. I know I didn't do so well."

He pursed his lips. "No, I'm afraid you didn't. I know you had some issues with our Shakespeare reading. You know I'm here if you need some extra help."

I nodded. "Yeah, I know," I said. "Honestly, I didn't remember we were having a test. I know I should have studied..." My voice sounded as pathetic as I felt. "I'm so sorry. I never got such a bad grade before. I promise I'll do better next time." I forced myself to look him in the eye so he knew I meant it. It was taking every ounce of willpower not to break down and tear the paper into little bits for being so embarrassing.

"You don't need to be sorry, but I will need you to get your parents to sign the test, okay? And don't forget, you'll have an opportunity to drop this mark with your media project!"

"Oh!" I said. Relief bubbled through me. "I totally forgot about that. That's great. I'm doing a documentary," I said. "It's going to be amazing, I promise. Do I still need to get the test signed? I mean, if I can win the free grade, then..."

"That sounds wonderful! With your grandfather, I'm not surprised you picked film," he replied. "But

I'm afraid your parents will still need to see and sign your test. Don't worry. We all have bad days."

I tried to shrug, but it came out all twitchy. Would my F make me look like an idiot to all my new teachers when I went to high school next year? Grown-ups were always talking about our grades in junior high and how a bad grade can follow us all through high school. I didn't want to look like a giant dumbo when I finally left eighth grade! And what about Kevin? I couldn't exactly have a super-genius boyfriend if I'm getting Fs!

Suddenly, my F felt like more than a test result.

F is for failure.

F is for fell flat on her face.

F is for fat chance on keeping your smart boyfriend, Ana.

I shook my head, trying to shake off the thought. "I'll get it signed," I said, sitting taller. "But I'm also going to win, so I can ditch this grade." I stuffed my test back into my pocket, eager to get it out of sight.

As I walked down the hallway, a twinge of doubt rang through me. One time when we were younger, I built a house of cards with Daz. We worked *so* hard to be super careful and had to get every card right so when we finally put that last card on the top it was perfect. *That's* how I felt working on my documentary now—like if I slipped up even once or made a wrong move, my life would plummet to the ground in a spectacular mess.

With Sugar's help, I would have to make a documentary that blew them all away. And with my friendship with Liv *and* my epic fail on the line, I couldn't mess up the tiniest thing.

After two days of getting off my skunk smell and convincing my parents that I wasn't on a downward spiral at school because of one Shakespeare test, it was finally time to hang out with Liv again. She'd spent a few days with her grandmother, and I was pretty excited to put boring school aside and tell her my story about the wildlife center. Something about facing off against wild skunks made me feel like even our busted-up friendship could be fixed.

Adjusting my sweater, I knocked on the door of her hotel room where she and her folks were staying for the rest of the week.

"Hey!" Liv exclaimed, opening the door. Her parents were gone, and she had her laptop splayed open on the bed. Loud, angsty music was pumping out of the speakers. "Come in!" she yelled over the noise. "I have Red Vines!" She helicoptered one in the air around her head.

I kicked off my shoes and collapsed onto the bed, already feeling buoyed by the smile on her face. Red Vines were a total Liv snack; I *knew* the real Liv was in there somewhere, buried beneath all that purple hair.

"How was your gram's?" I asked, reaching for some candy.

She clicked the music down on her laptop, shrugging. "Oh, you know," she replied. "Same old grammie. Still asking why we had to move away. Still makes the world's hardest oatmeal cookies." Her eyes rolled. "I think I chipped a tooth."

I giggled. "It's nice to know that some things don't change."

Liv sprawled out on the bed beside me, tucking her hair behind her ears. The dragon wrapped around her ear stared at me with its tiny, judgmental, ruby eyes. "Whatever," she said coolly. "She also said she hated my hair, so that was nice."

I stopped eating, mid-chew. Part of me was a little pleased that *someone* had spoken up about Liv's hair. But the other part of me hated seeing Liv act so...*cold*. She used to love visiting her grammie and would even complain if her parents had to leave early from their visit. Now she was acting like it was the world's biggest inconvenience to see her?

I frowned, mentally checking off one more change in Liv's attitude since her return. It was almost like she was trying to be as different as possible, just to freak me out.

"So what did you do?" She rolled from the bed and reached into the mini fridge under the TV. "Want a Diet Coke?" she asked, handing me one.

"Aren't those things crazy expensive?" I asked. Every time my parents and I stayed in a hotel, we (and by *we*, I mean Daz) were strictly forbidden from opening the mini fridges. Dad always said he isn't going to pay six dollars for something that cost thirty cents to make.

She rolled her eyes. "You sound like my parents," she said, sighing. "They told me not to have anything from in here, but come on, if *you're* here, they can hardly get me in trouble." She reached for a second can and cracked the lid open with her dark-purple nails, sending a fizzy burst up to her nose as she took a sip.

The sound seemed louder than it should.

Then she sniffed the air. "Do you smell that?"

Hesitantly, I took the can. My stomach was already in knots, and I'd only been in the room for five minutes. I tried to casually lean my head down to sniff myself. I didn't still reek, did I?

"So, a while ago, this fox got hit by a car," I said,

shimmying closer on the bed to grab another Red Vine. I waited a beat for Liv to react—she used to love animals and visiting Mom at her lion exhibit— but her face stayed the same.

"And then I went in with Mom to the zoo while they worked on him, and eventually he got sent to this cool wildlife rescue center, where they help all sorts of animals so they can be released again. And guess what!" I said, trying to force a little too much enthusiasm into my voice to make up for Liv's dead-pan face.

"They released him?" she asked, her eyes brightening. She took another sniff of the air, her nose crinkling. "Seriously, what is that smell?"

I grinned. "I'm getting to that. They didn't release him yet. *But* I got to go in and actually volunteer there! I got to work with *real* wild animals, that are actually going to get to go back into the forest once they're better!"

Finally, *finally* Liv seemed to snap out of her weird emo mood. The spark returned to her eyes. "For real?! That's so cool, Ana! It's like the zoo, only even *wilder*!" She sat on her heels, stuffing another licorice in her mouth.

I beamed, my heart filling with relief to see her act like her old excited self. "That's exactly what *I* thought! It was the coolest thing. I mean, I totally got sprayed by a skunk, but how cool is it to get to help these animals get healthy again, right?"

Liv's jaw dropped. "So it's *you*!" She grabbed a pillow and smacked me on the head with it. "You're what stinks in here!"

I frowned. "It's almost gone!" I cried, grabbing a handful of hair and leaning closer so she could smell it, to gross her out further. "I had to shower until we ran out of hot water! It used to be *horrible*."

Liv shoved me away, laughing. "You talk about some things never changing," she cackled. "You always were the stinkiest kid in school!"

I shoved her back with the pillow and giggled, sticking out my tongue in false protest. "Well, we can't both be known as the girl with purple hair!" I closed my eyes for a brief moment, secretly thanking the Red Vine gods for their help.

This is how I wanted everything to go when Liv first came back. Maybe Liv had been having a bad couple of days when we hung out before? My insides were jittery with happiness, seeing her act like her usual goofbally self.

She's back! She's back! She's normal Liv again!

Just then, a loud ringing started to sound from her laptop. Scrambling to her feet, she yanked it onto her lap.

"It's Leilani!" she squealed. Her eyebrows lifted

hopefully. "Do you want to talk to her? Let's talk to her! I told her to call if she could!"

Instantly, the glee inside me was squashed, like it had been sat on by a giant elephant.

An elephant named Leilani.

She *told* her to call? When she knew I'd be here?

I hardly ever got to see Liv now, and here was Leilani interrupting our day *again*. But I didn't want to seem like a jerk, so I pretended I didn't care. If our friendship was going to be okay, I would have to learn to deal with Liv's other friends.

"Sure," I said, stuffing down my disappointment. "Sounds good."

Nope. Nope. Nope.

Casually smoothing down my hair from our pillow fight, I held my breath as Liv propped up her laptop on a pillow and clicked the video chat button.

"Heyyyyyy!" she said, dragging her voice out in a whine. She waved to the screen.

You know, I've seen some pretty fast things happen. I've seen snakes snap at their keepers at the zoo, and I've even seen sharks snap at each other at lightning speed. But none of that was as fast as Liv's demeanor shifting when she clicked that one little button.

Instead of her usual, bubbly self, she had rearranged her face to look sort of…unimpressed? Snarky? Her wide smile was replaced with a wry one, like she was keeping some joke a secret and wasn't about to tell anyone the punch line.

It made my stomach turn. Was *this* why Liv was acting so weird and mood-swingy?

"Olive!" The voice on the screen echoed her.

Olive? I made a face at Liv, lifting my hands in question. *Who the heck was Olive?*

"What's up?" Liv asked, gesturing for me to come join her. But for some reason, I was sort of scared to face Leilani now. It made her seem that much more real. I took my time rolling from the other side of the bed around to where Liv was sitting.

Leilani, on the other hand, was talking a mile a minute now. "I miss you," she said, whining.

I bit my lip to keep from smiling. She thought *she* missed Liv? Welcome to *my* life, Leilani.

"Plus, I was talking to Becky, and she told me that Dan told her that Ryan said *he* missed you," she said.

My memory flickered. Ryan was the greasy-looking kid in the photo Liv had shown me, right? Barf.

But I didn't say that. Instead, I put on a supportive face and gave her a thumbs-up. *Be a good friend, Ana.*

"Really?!" Liv asked, wriggling with excitement. "That's amazing! I wish I were there right now!"

Her words hit me like a swarm of wasps. *Say what?* She wished she were back in New Zealand all because of some skuzzy guy? Since when was Liv so boy crazy?

"Come here!" she hissed, snapping me out of my mental rant. "Lei, this is Ana. I've told you about her!"

Liv yanked me closer, in view of the screen. Taking a nervous breath, I put on my absolute coolest face, trying to look like those girls do in the yogurt commercials where they look all carefree and chill with their little spoons and hips shaking everywhere.

"Hey, Leilani," I said, smiling. "It's great to meet you!" I lifted my hand in a super-casual wave.

I swear, I should have gotten an Oscar for this performance.

The girl's eyes narrowed for a moment, like she was inspecting a shirt at the store but wasn't sure if she wanted to buy it yet. I'd seen that face on Ashley a hundred times.

"She doesn't *look* like a celebrity," Leilani said, her lips curling into a sneer. And trust me, I *know* sneers. This sneer was level three, with some fake laughter thrown in so the sneeree would take it like a joke. My hands clenched into fists at my side.

"I'm not a celebrity," I said, glancing at Liv. I kept my twitchy smile firmly plastered onto my face. So far, I could tell by the little image of me in the corner that my ears were turning pink. But I would *not* let Leilani shake me up.

"Sure you are!" Liv said, eyes widening. "She's going to be in a documentary and everything. You should be here today," she added. "She smells like skunk. We need smell-ternet."

"Ew!" Leilani said, backing away from her screen. "That's disgusting."

I pursed my lips, trying to think of the perfect comeback.

At least my hair doesn't look ridiculous.

At least I don't look like I'm about to rob a bank.

At least I've been friends with Liv for almost a decade and you've only known her a few months, so HA.

And then, right when I thought Liv was going to stand up for me and say that it wasn't that bad or that it was cool because it meant I got to work at a wildlife center, she said, "Right?! She has a reputation for being the smelly one! She lived in the zoo, remember?"

Leilani cackled as I glared at Liv. I mean, sure. It was technically true, but when she had mentioned me always stinking from something zoo-related five minutes ago, it seemed like she meant it in an endearing way. *This*, though? This sounded mean.

"Is she the one who had that wacky allergic reaction to Nair you were telling me about?" Leilani giggled.

I clamped my mouth shut, shocked. Had Liv actually *told* Leilani about my horrible Nair day? That wasn't *wacky*—that was terrifying! I'd spent all afternoon covered in painful welts. I couldn't believe Liv had told her that. You don't tell random people about your best friend's most embarrassing moments. You *especially* don't tell people about them in a way that makes them *laugh*.

Suddenly, I couldn't see straight. "Sorry, I think I gotta go," I mumbled. "I totally forgot I have to be home by six to help with dinner."

Rushing over to my backpack, I cringed at the sight of my video camera, clipped to the side in its own squishy bag. I'd wanted to shoot some stuff with Liv for my documentary, but the hollow feeling in my stomach made that the last thing on my mind. All I wanted was to show Liv how much she meant to be as a friend, and here she was being a total flake to me with stupid Leilani. I wasn't even sure if I *wanted* to include her in it right now.

"See you later though, right?" Liv asked, looking up from the screen.

I nodded brusquely, bending over to tie my boots. Refusing to let her see me upset, I plastered on another tight smile. "Yup, the party is tomorrow," I reminded her. "If your parents want to drop you off at the zoo, you can stay the night," I mumbled.

She tilted her head. "What party?" she asked, furrowing her brow.

My body went cold.

"What?!" I asked, not caring how shrill I sounded. "You're kidding, right?"

The blank look on her face gutted me. I couldn't believe it.

"You forgot," I said, avoiding her eyes. I tightened the straps of my backpack and rushed for the door. I yanked it open, nearly smacking myself in the face with it. "You forgot my birthday."

"Ana! Wait!"

I was in the elevator by the time she caught up to me. Wiping my eyes angrily on my sleeve, I shook my head. "It's fine," I said. "You've been busy."

Busy being somebody I don't even recognize.

Liv scoffed. Clearly my attempt to sound normal wasn't working. "I'm sorry, okay! Leilani was asking me yesterday about an audition at home and it's the same date, and I got sidetracked. I'll be at your party, duh. What time should I show up?"

"It's at—" I stopped short, dots connecting in my head. I knew Ashley had to leave the party early for a swim meet at two o'clock. The party started at one o'clock, so if Liv was a little bit later, I wouldn't have to worry about the two of them meeting. Could I risk another rift between us, now that she'd basically shown me she *forgot* something so important to me? Not to mention she had practically *dragged* Leilani into our day *again*.

My heart hurt too much to risk it.

I couldn't let our friendship keep cracking like this.

"Two o'clock," I said firmly. "It starts at two."

"I'll be there! And, hey," Liv said. "I'm sorry. I totally knew it was your birthday. I just got distracted. Okay?"

I nodded numbly. "Okay," I said. But nothing about what I was feeling was *okay*. Sure, sometimes friends did dumb things to each other, but you only needed to talk it out and you felt better. But what are you supposed to do when it's a zillion *tiny* things— being weird, being mean, being just plain *different*— and it feels impossible to tell them exactly what's bugging you because you can't find the words?

"Good," she said. She trotted back to her hotel room while I pushed the button on the elevator.

I waited for the doors to close before the tears started up.

Chapter 13

Buried beneath the snow, hibernating wood frogs can survive being frozen solid. Their hearts even stop beating. When the weather warms up again, they simply thaw out and get back to business.

—Animal Wisdom

Imagine being a frogsicle and getting to hide all winter! I bet they wake up with some horrible pins and needles though.

There are days you wake up and *know* things are different. Your bed feels weird. Your pillow won't fluff right no matter how many times you punch it. Your best friend forgot your birthday for the first time ever.

And your idiot brother won't leave you alone for ten minutes to let you wake up in the morning like a normal person.

"Wake up! Wake up! Wake up!" Daz screeched. "I am thirteen today! *We* are thirteen todayyyy!" He hopped on my desk and leaped over my bed. The springs creaked angrily as he kept bouncing.

"Gah, Daz!" I growled, throwing my covers off with a huff. Darwin flapped his wings in annoyance. "Get *out*!"

"What do you think we got for presents?!" He catapulted over me to land on the floor with a somersault. I had no idea how Daz managed to not break his face doing these stunts of his, but one thing was clear—he had definitely sneaked some coffee this morning.

"A robot servant!" I yelled, joining him by jumping on the bed. "Mom told me not to tell you!"

He stopped short. "Wait," he said. His eyes widened, and he jumped up beside me. "Are you serious? Because I have been *asking*—" The joy in his eyes was hilarious to see. It was exactly what I needed after my awful night yesterday.

"Nope!" I yelped, diving away from him to avoid his reach. "You're getting gullible in your old age, loser!"

I cackled as I ran down the hallway in my socked feet, sliding on the pine floors. For a moment, I thought maybe Daz and I had switched bodies on our birthday, like in that movie with Lindsay Lohan and that pretty older lady. But if I couldn't tease my brother on my own birthday, then what was the point, right? Even a bad night with Liv couldn't change the fact: I was *thirteen* today. I was officially a teenager!

"Good morning, my little birthday girl!" Dad greeted me in the kitchen with a plateful of pancakes. Sliced strawberries and bananas looked back at me in a fruity happy face. He set the plate on the table and wrapped me in a huge hug.

"I can't believe my peanut is thirteen. It seems like only yesterday we were bringing you guys home from the hospital," he said, ruffling my hair. I squirmed from the hair noogie, but deep down I was enjoying the feeling of being a teenager already. Even my *cells* felt older. Do your insides know when you become a teenager too?

Mom joined in, moving fast enough to wrangle Daz in a hug. "It was so nice of that random woman to leave you guys in the waiting room for us," she joked.

"Thanks," I said, sliding into my chair at the table. I took a deep breath as I stared at my breakfast, doing my best to remember this moment. As much as my mind kept drifting to Liv, I didn't want my whole day to suck. I wouldn't turn thirteen again for the rest of my whole *life*, so I wanted to make sure I wouldn't forget any of it, you know? The pancakes, the berries, the way the sun was streaming in through the windows, and even the cold chill on the tips of my toes from the floor.

"Waiting for them to ask you to eat them?" Daz asked, plunking down next to me with his own plate. It was piled high with pancakes, along with a huge well of syrup that was dangerously close to slopping over the edge.

"I'm *remembering* the moment. We aren't all cavemen," I said haughtily. "Do you realize this is the *only* time in your entire life you're going to turn thirteen." I started cutting my pancakes into bite-sized pieces, sliding one through my pool of syrup with my fork.

"Not true," Daz said, shoveling a huge bite into his mouth. His cheeks were stretched full like a chipmunk. "Mex fear ve be furdeen pus won!"

He chomped happily as Mom and Dad sat down to join us. A spark of excitement surged through me to see they had tucked a few shiny presents under their feet.

"Huh?" I said, edging away from Daz's soon-to-be spit shower. "Please don't mention pus at the table."

He swallowed his bite. "Not true," he repeated. "This isn't the only time in our lives we'll be turning thirteen." He leaned over and poked me in the arm with his fork. "*Think*." Then he tapped the same fork on his forehead to make his point, nearly taking out an eyeball.

I stared at him, silently trying to compute how he could be right. "There's no way," I said finally. "This is *it*, this moment here, and you're ruining it by eating like a monkey."

"Next year," he said, jabbing his fork into another stack of pancakes. "We'll be turning *thirteen plus one*. Thirteen will be *in* us, for the rest of our *liiiiiives*!" he bellowed, narrowing his eyes and taking aim at a strawberry on the edge of my plate.

I rolled my eyes at him, but I couldn't help but feel a little comforted by the fact that maybe thirteen wasn't as final as I thought. Not that I was going to admit that to the Pancake Monster pigging out beside me. Sometimes, when Daz makes me actually *think* I worry that he might secretly be a genius.

That would be so unfair.

"Strawberry *deaaath*," he murmured, mashing his berries into his pancake.

Then again, maybe not.

"So," Mom said. Her voice was full of mystery. "We know you guys have your party later today, but your dad and I wanted to give you our presents early, before everyone else."

"*Yeth!*" Daz squealed through a mouthful. He raised his fork in the air like a victory move.

"Maybe after you finish eating," Dad said wisely.

"Done!" Daz said, piling the last of his pancake into his mouth. I swear, I know we're supposed to be twins and all that, but honestly if I ate as much as Daz did, I would probably be about the size of a hippo. Why didn't he have to worry about fitting into his pants, when my pants seemed to get tighter when I even *looked* at a cookie?

Mom handed me a box wrapped in lime-green paper. It was the same color as the T-shirts we wear at the zoo. A smaller yellow box was tucked on the top, nearly hidden by a gigantic orange ribbon.

"These are for you, Ana," she said.

Daz's fingers wriggled excitedly as Mom handed him his gifts, a box wrapped in red paper and a smaller silvery gift bag.

"Ladies first," Dad said, gesturing to me. "She was born a whole four minutes earlier, after all." He winked at Mom.

Even though I was dying to rip open the paper first, I started with the card. If there's one thing that being thirteen has taught me it's that you have to do the mature thing, even if there are presents sitting in front of you.

Usually, my parents get us jokey cards. You know, with monkeys and bananas on the front or pigs dressed up in sunglasses and bow ties. But this one was more artistic and serious, like someone had hand drawn it. A girl in charcoal stared back at me, with a gray parrot sitting on her shoulder.

"That's me!" I said, clutching the card. "Who drew this?" I inspected the bottom of the picture, and instantly my heart leaped. A bold "S. F." was scribbled in the corner. "Shep Foster! Grandpa made this!" I held out the card for Daz to see.

Mom nodded. "He did one for each of you guys, to go with our presents," she said. "We can't draw, but he used to. Just like you, kiddo."

I nodded. I still had the sketchbook that Grandpa had given me in the summer, full of his sketches and doodles. That was back when I thought we had nothing in common.

I read the inside of the card.

To our dearest Ana,

Words cannot express how incredibly proud we are to have you as our daughter, and watching you grow up to be a beautiful, intelligent young lady is one of the greatest gifts in our lives. Enjoy your special day!

Love always,
Mom and Dad

Usually, I wasn't one for serious cards. But this one seemed different. I made a mental note to put it someplace special. A lump formed in my throat as I turned to the presents.

Tugging off the paper from the smaller box, I grinned with delight. "Art supplies!" I squealed.

Daz peered over my shoulder as I tore away the last of the paper and opened the box. Inside was a gorgeous wooden box, sanded down to a smooth, tawny finish. Lifting the top gingerly, I gasped at all the colors. A whole rainbow of possibilities stared back me.

"You guys! This is awesome! *Everything* is in here!" I pointed out the beautiful pastels, pencil crayons, charcoals, and oil paints. It even had water-color pencils that you can only use on special paper.

"You haven't had much time to doodle lately with school, but we know how happy it makes you," Mom said, reaching around to hug me. "Never lose your creative spirit," she whispered. "No matter what you do in life, okay? Maybe you could sketch some of the new animals at Safe Haven!"

I nodded. Already I couldn't wait to make something. What was it about a box of fresh art supplies that made you feel like you fit the whole world inside your heart?

I squirmed with excitement as I moved on to the

second box. This one was much bigger than the first and a little bit heavier.

"I hope they fit…" Mom said eagerly. Panic rose in my chest as I wondered what "they" could mean. Pants? *Bras?* She wouldn't get me bras, would she? In front of Daz?!

But I didn't have to worry.

Instead of embarrassing bras, a brand-new pair of beautiful brown leather boots with purple laces stared up at me. They weren't fancy boots with heels, like some of the girls in school wear. But they also weren't boring old work boots like my dad wears. They were perfect and in between, with a teensy bit of heel on the back so they looked polished and extra special.

"Ooh." I breathed, running my hand over the soft leather. "I *love* them!" I looked up to Mom and Dad, who were now holding hands. Something about their kids getting old must make parents extra schmoopy around each other.

"See if they fit!" Dad said. "They should be the right size, and we picked up those laces for you. We also got you green ones, so you can switch them as you like."

Mom's smile widened. "We wanted something that you could wear every day, not only for special occasions," she said.

I pulled one out of the box and stuck in my bare foot. The sole was extra squishy, like walking on a marshmallow. "They fit!" I exclaimed.

And they looked *good*.

I laced it up to the top, where they just covered my ankle. Mom was right—they would be perfect for wearing with jeans, but they were also nice enough that I could look a little extra special, if I wanted to. Buoyed with how awesome I already felt, I laced the second one up. They even looked good with my penguin pajamas on, *that's* how cool they were.

"When I was thirteen, my father gave me a special pair of boots too," Mom said.

"He did?" I asked. It was so hard to picture Grandpa having a thirteen-year-old daughter. Almost as hard as it was to picture my own *mother* being thirteen.

Her eyes shone. "He believes that every young woman should have something great to wear on her feet while she climbs mountains and conquers the world," she said, blinking back her tears. "Your dad and I happen to agree."

"Thanks, you guys," I said. I stood up to give them a hug. I may not have been able to conquer the world, but I was definitely feeling more prepared for thirteen in these boots. Maybe even strong enough to finish my documentary, get an A plus, and fix my friendship with Liv.

I kept my boots on while Daz opened his gifts and hooted up a storm when he saw Mom and Dad had gotten him a year's subscription to *RobotWorld* magazine—the world's leading magazine for robot-loving, techie weirdos like my brother, I guess? He also got an engraved pocketknife, which, if you ask *me*, was asking for a trip to the ER, but it's his eyeball, not mine.

When we were done with presents and breakfast, I undid my new boots and set them beside my bed. Darwin hopped down from my desk to check them out. I almost didn't want to have a birthday party today. Instead, I could spend the whole day trying out my art supplies.

My phone buzzed beside me.

"*Birthday banana!*" Darwin crowed, hopping onto my shoulder. He watched intently as I checked my phone, reaching to peck at Ashley's face on the screen. Her message was blinking impatiently.

Ash: HAPPY BIRTHDAY, WEIRDO! I was going to call you Scales, but it IS your birthday, after all, so I decided to be nice. You'd better not eat all the cake before I get there!

I grinned, then realized that this was actually the first text I'd received today. Usually, Liv sent me a birthday email, loaded with pictures of cute kittens and pizza. But Ashley's message was the only thing in my inbox. So I guess not everything magically got better when you turned thirteen, after all.

"I did the right thing, Dar," I said, leaning my head into his. "Liv and I seem barely friends at all right now. I can't risk anything else bad."

"*Disaster banana!*" he agreed. At least, I *think* he agreed.

Typing into my phone, I let him nibble at my fingers.

AnaBanana: I'll save you a corner piece with all the icing! Still have to leave early?

Say yes, say yes.

Darwin hopped onto my desk as I drummed my fingers impatiently on my leg.

"What are you looking at?" I challenged him. "Liv *forgot* my birthday. Do you really think having her mortal enemy nearby will help?" I narrowed my eyes at him.

My phone beeped again.

Ash: Yeah, sorry!

I slumped with relief.

"Time to make myself look thirteen," I told him. Leaving him to inspect my new boots, I gave myself one last pep-talk-y look in the mirror and headed for the shower. Cake would make everything better, right?

Top Three Weirdest Things about Being Thirteen

1. Although I don't *look* any different, I definitely feel different. I mean, was I hoping to wake up and look in the mirror and see supermodel boobs staring back at me? Sure. But I'm still me, and it's probably better to have no surprises on a day like today, rather than be wondering how I'm going to fit in all my old bras, right? Yes, that's me doing my best to find a silver lining, but deal with it.

2. What was I saying again? Right, *feeling* different. Although it could be the pancakes and strawberries talking, I do feel a little older. Like my skin is stretching and my insides are bursting out. That probably sounds like a horrible disease, but maybe that's one of the things grown-ups are always talking about when they say teenagers are weird. Really, we're walking around practically bursting out of our skins doing our best to keep ourselves together against all the craziness in our heads.

3. The way your parents stare at you all dreamy-eyed with this faraway look in their eyes. I asked Mom why she and Dad kept doing it to me, and all she said was "Oh, honey, time flies, that's all," with this sad little smile. When exactly does time start flying exactly? When I'm twenty? Thirty? Because I don't know about you, but there are about a million and a half reasons I would like time to fly (like when I'm stuck in the cafeteria line), and all I can tell is that this world doesn't speed up for anyone.

Chapter 14

Coyotes are one of the most adaptable animals on the planet, surviving in almost every biome. They live in every state, except Hawaii.

—*Animal Wisdom*

Poor coyotes. All those states and they don't get to live in the one on all the postcards with fancy beaches and sunsets.

I. Am. Thirteen.

It's funny. You can go ages thinking you have only a few friends at school, but then suddenly you offer up some free birthday cake and ice cream and the whole world shows up, ready to high-five you and hand you presents.

I'd been thirteen for only a few hours so far, but already it was turning into one of the *coolest* years of my life. Was it too early to say that? All I knew was that the banquet hall of the zoo was jam-packed with kids, most of whom were super eager to give me presents, cards, and even hugs.

A huge table of snacks was arranged at the side of the room, with trays of veggies and dip, mini sandwiches, chips, punch, and cans of soda perched on top of a bright purple-and-green tablecloth. Happy-looking balloons and streamers were scattered all over the room, dancing in the breeze as people opened and closed the door. And in the corner, a six-foot-tall inflatable dinosaur manned the bathroom door.

I grinned, happy that Daz was able to have a dinosaur at the party after all.

"Pretty great turnout, right?" Bella came up to me and wrapped me up in a hug. "Happy birthday!" My heart warmed to see that she had purple-and-green clips in her hair to match the decorations.

Bouncing on my heels, I nodded. "It's amazing! I never knew so many people would come!" I pointed out the group of guys standing by the punch bowl. Eric, also known as The Guy Who Wears Too Much Cologne, was goofing off with Zack. "Even *Zack* came." I made a face. He and Eric kept sneaking glances at Sugar, who was talking animatedly with Grandpa a few tables away.

Bella laughed. "Well, to be fair, they're probably here for the free pizza," she said. "No offense," she added quickly.

"Daz probably invited them," I said, nodding. Maybe twelve-year-old Ana might be annoyed to see such a jerk at *my* birthday party (*he* was the reason I got covered in chicken parm in the cafeteria last year), but thirteen-year-old Ana knew that sometimes guys were idiots and the best thing you could do was ignore them.

Sort of like mosquitoes.

Or the calorie count of s'mores.

"When do you think Liv will get here?" Bella asked, checking her watch. "She's a bit late..."

Instantly, my throat tightened. I hadn't exactly told Bella about my plan to keep Liv and Ashley apart, mainly because when I thought about saying it out loud, it seemed a *lot* worse than it actually was.

"Um," I said, checking my own watch. "I think she mentioned she might be a little late." The tally of lies that was building in my head rang off with a warning ding.

Lies to Bella: one.

"Oh!" Bella exclaimed suddenly. "There she is!" She gripped my arm and pointed to the door.

"*What?!*" I whirled around, cursing myself already for sounding *wayyyy* too shocked. But Liv wasn't supposed to be here yet! She was supposed to come in twenty minutes, after Ashley left!

"Let's go say hey," she said, starting to lift her hand in a wave.

And I almost waved alongside her.

That is, until I saw Ashley appear from behind the snack table, with a cup of punch in her hand.

I sucked in a breath and ducked my head behind a cluster of green balloons in the corner, yanking Bella with me. "Can you do me a favor?" I whispered to Bella as I peeked around the corner. It's crazy how a room can seem inviting and happy one minute and like a viper's nest the next. I *couldn't* let Liv see Ashley, not like this.

"Um, okay?" Bella said. Her mouth formed a thin line. "Are you all right? You look…green." She darted a look around us. "Is it Zack? Do you want me to see if we can get him to leave or something?" Her voice was hushed, like she didn't want me to be embarrassed by it.

I shook my head. "It's not that," I hissed. I peeked out again. Liv was talking to Daz now, scanning the room. I could tell by the question in her eyes that she was looking for me. "Would you mind talking to Liv for a few minutes? I have a"—my mind raced—"a *surprise* for her. And I don't want her to see it yet!"

God, I am such a horrible person.

Bella's eyes lit up. "Oh! Uh…okay, I guess," she said slowly. "I mean, you know I don't know her very well, right? So it might be a little weird if I walk up and start to—"

"That's all right," I said, cutting her off. I made a promise to myself that I'd explain everything to Bella when I wasn't in crisis mode like this. It felt like two planets were about to collide with each other. I'd seen enough of the PBS channel to know what happened when planets collided—*worlds* ended.

"She won't mind! Maybe keep her in here, by the snacks!" Checking my watch, I calculated how much time was left before Ashley needed to leave. "I'll be like ten minutes, swear! Ask her about New Zealand. She loves that!"

Bella nodded but gave me one last look of confusion before making her way to Liv. Relief poured through me as Bella stood between us, blocking Liv's view of me. Stuffing my hands into my pockets, I made a beeline for Ashley.

I had to get her out of here.

"Hey!" I said, forcing my voice to sound as casual as possible. "Having fun?" I edged forward slowly, trying to herd Ashley toward the side exit.

"There you are!" She took one more sip of punch and wiped her mouth daintily with a napkin. For a moment, she looked as nervous as I *felt*. "You have a minute?" she asked. "I have a present for you, but it's embarrassing and cheesy." She tapped her foot impatiently as she glanced awkwardly around her at the crowd.

"Yes!" I said, grateful for the excuse to head outside away from Liv. "Let's get some air."

I ducked out the side exit, following Ashley out of the visitor's center. It occurred to me that not so long ago, an invitation like this from Ashley would have probably left me running for the hills. It's funny how much our lives can change without us noticing it.

"What's up?" I asked. Already the weight on my shoulders felt lighter, and I was able to suck in a deep breath. Liv was inside. Ashley was outside. It was all fine.

Better than fine.

I grinned as Ashley handed me a small, silvery box tied tight with a blue ribbon.

"What's this?" I asked. I know that you're probably supposed to expect presents on your birthday, but if Past Ana could see me actually getting a *gift* from Ashley, she would probably flip her biscuit.

"What do you *think* it is?! It's for your birthday!

Open it!" Ashley said. Her smile was tight with excitement as she rubbed her hands together. The wind picked up, sending her hair cascading over her shoulders in a breezy wave.

I tugged the thin blue ribbon around the box. It wasn't heavy, which made me even more nervous. Carefully lifting the lid, I peeked inside and pulled out some of the icy-blue tissue paper.

"The lady at the gift shop wrapped it," she said, wringing her hands. "Hurry *uuuppp!*"

Finally, I dug through the paper to find a teensy silver cord. A silver crocodile was attached to it, topped with a glittery green gemstone.

"It's beautiful!" I gaped. "Is it a necklace?" I gingerly lifted it out of the box. The silver sparkled in the midday autumn sun.

"A bracelet," she said. "I saw it in the zoo gift shop, and I knew I had to get it for you. I mean, it's a crocodile and all. Don't feel too special though." She lifted her arm to show off a gold bracelet. A teensy gold shark glittered back at me. "I got one too. A shark, obviously." She clicked her tongue.

"I love it!" She helped me do up the teensy clasp. It was the perfect size, not too big and not extra dangly so I'd be getting it caught in everything. My heart squeezed with happiness.

"We match," Ashley said, lifting her eyebrows.

"Never thought *that* would happen, huh? You have to admit, sharks are better, but—"

My stomach dropped as the lighthearted look in Ashley's eyes morphed into one of shock.

"What?" I whirled around to follow her gaze, but it only took a nanosecond to see what had Ashley so surprised.

My blood turned to ice.

Liv was staring at us, her mouth dropped open.

Chapter 15

Night snakes are rear fanged, which means their fangs are located at the back of their mouths instead of the front.

—*Animal Wisdom*

Great. So not only are there snakes with nasty, obvious fangs, there are also snakes with secret, hidden fangs. There's a surprise I don't want to get, thankyouverymuch.

Liv was ten feet away, but she was already stumbling back. Her fists were clenched, and her eyebrows were knit together in a harsh, dark line. "What the *hell*, Ana?" she spat. Her eyes darted back and forth from me to Ashley.

I tried to open my mouth to speak, but the spazzy fear had already taken me over. Behind Liv, Bella was standing like she'd seen a ghost. Her mouth hung open in a tiny *O*, and her eyes were full of questions.

Just keep it *together*.

My thoughts whizzed around like a balloon with the air let out of it. This was a silly misunderstanding, and there was no way I could let it ruin everything. I just had to think of something that made perfect sense.

"Liv! Hi!" I said, waving her over. *Play it cool.* "We were—"

"No, I think I pretty much have it figured out. You guys *match*. Why did you lie to me, Ana? I *asked* you!" I could tell from the way Liv's fingers clenched and unclenched that she was trying desperately not to cry in front of us. It was the same thing she had done when her goldfish died in fifth grade, and the same thing she had done when her mom convinced her to get a perm in second grade that made her look like a fuzzy Pomeranian.

It made my heart ache. But *she* was the one who had been acting so weird and making me feel like our friendship was hanging by a thread!

"I didn't lie! I—"

"Stop it!" She cut me off again, her voice getting higher and squeakier. "Is *this* why you told me not to show up until two o'clock? So I wouldn't know you were best buddies with *stupid Sneerer Ashley*?! It's probably why you sent *Bella* to talk with me! To keep me occupied?!"

"Whoa, now," Ashley said, taking a step back. She scoffed and turned to me expectantly, the fire in her eyes practically burning me. She held her hands up too, which didn't help matters because her shark bracelet was *still* the only thing I could see.

And I'm pretty sure it was the only thing Liv could see too.

"Can we please talk?" I begged. I *knew* how awful it looked. How would I feel if I'd caught Leilani giving a friendship bracelet to Liv? It was bad enough they texted every waking moment. But it *wasn't* like that! I was trying to *save* our friendship, not ruin it!

"Why don't you just admit it?!" Liv seethed. Her face was flushed, and her voice was as sharp as glass.

My throat ached. In all the years we'd been best friends, I couldn't remember a *single* time when she'd glared at me with such hate in her eyes. Not even when I ruined her favorite blue sweater by accidentally spilling fake blood on it at Halloween.

Despite what I'd done, had *so* much changed between us in such a short time that she could seriously hate me?

"You lied to me about not being friends with Ashley, and you let me go on and on about her when we talk, all the while sneaking around and hanging out together behind my back! And now this!" She lashed out, pointing at my bracelet. It felt like a chain, pulling me down into the ground, instead of a beautiful gift. "Why didn't you tell me from the start?"

"I tried," I croaked. "But every time I did, something happened, and I didn't want you to get upset, especially since things are sort of weird between us. And Leilani—" My throat was dry, with every little breath tearing at me from the inside.

Please, *please* don't do this.

Liv shook her head. "I wonder why *that* is! And *don't* even mention Leilani! I never lied to you about anything! It's not my fault she's a better friend than *you* are right now," she snapped, glaring at Ashley. Then she dug into her jacket pocket and pulled out a small present wrapped in purple paper.

She had gotten me a *present*.

My heart squeezed, desperate to turn back time so this whole mess hadn't happened.

"It's nothing special," she said. Her lip was quivering, and I could tell she was doing everything she could to stop from crying. "It's not some fancy documentary or a silver bracelet or anything some *celebrity* would want with their awesome *new life*," she choked out, wiping her nose on her sleeve angrily, tossing the present at my feet. It landed with a clatter onto the dead, brown grass. As she turned her heel and started to stomp away, she nearly plowed into Bella.

Tears stung in my eyes as I stood, staring after Liv and sniffling like an idiot. What the heck happened to us?! We were supposed to be friends! Liv and I had fought before, but this felt different. Friends didn't run off when things got sucky.

Friends *listened* to each other.

They give each other a chance.

Beside me, Ashley was shaking her head. "That was *low*, Ana," she said bitterly. "You're not going to have *any* friends if you keep treating them like that."

I wiped my eyes as I picked up Liv's gift, tearing off the wrapping. An old picture—the two of us at my first-grade birthday party, beaming and hanging off each other wearing matching pink feather boas—stared back at me. A sob caught in my throat. How could two people who used to be so close end up so broken?

"I'm so sorry, guys." I sniffled. "I didn't know what else to do, and everything's been so bad since Liv got here. I...I'm sorry. I won't put you in the middle like that again."

Bella sighed, shoulders slumped. "I don't *mind* being in the middle," she said. "That's what friends are for. But lying to us is pretty awful."

"I promise I won't do it again," I vowed. And honestly, I meant it.

"You better not," Ashley said. Her voice was tight, but I could tell by the way her face softened that she didn't hate me. At least I hoped so.

"Forgive me?" I asked.

Ashley scoffed. "Oh, go *get* her," she urged. "Yes, I forgive you. But standing here and snotting all over yourself isn't going to fix anything, right?"

Ashley was right. Apologizing again to both of them, I sucked in a breath and took off in a run.

I had to catch up with her.

I had to talk to her.

I had to save *us*.

"Liv!" I shouted. "Wait up!" I scrambled over the cobblestone, nearly twisting my ankle in the process. Leaping over an empty bench, I tried to take a shortcut through a mulched garden area to cut her off before she made it past the penguin exhibit. I couldn't let our friendship break like this. I had to figure out a way to be friends with everyone—and a *good* friend too—without lying or losing anyone along the way.

And you know what?

It might have actually worked if my left shoelace hadn't come untied.

Instead of sailing over the bench gracefully, my lace caught in one of the teensy slots between the wood. My shoe stayed put, but the yank from the stuck lace was enough to turn my attempt at a Superman impression into more of a clumsy flamingo. I toppled to the ground, landing on my wrist.

Cra-a-a-c-k!

The sick crunch seemed to echo through me. Had I broken the bench? Stars popped in my vision, and my head felt like it weighed as much as an elephant. I was going to throw up. I tried to shove myself up from my face-plant position to turn back and look, but my arm wouldn't cooperate. A sharp, icy pain shot through me.

"*Oww!*" I fumbled on my elbow. Something was wrong. Something was *definitely* wrong. Wrists shouldn't feel like this.

"Hey, loser!" Daz yelled from beside the hyenas. He was standing next to Kevin with an armful of presents. Concern clouded his face as he realized that I wasn't fooling around. The panicked, terrified look on my face probably tipped him off.

"Are you okay? Mom! Come 'ere!" he yelped, rushing over to me. Behind me, Ashley rounded the corner where I'd just become the worst stuntwoman in history.

Daz, Mom, and Ashley all knelt beside me, while Kevin stood a few feet away. Mom's face was white, but she spoke fast. "Okay, hun. Where does it hurt?" Her lips squished together as she gingerly pulled up my sleeve to inspect my wrist. I'd seen her make the same face when she was inspecting the fox for injuries. Was I broken like him? I *felt* like I'd been hit by a truck.

My stomach turned as I saw how angry and swollen my wrist looked already.

Ouch, ouch, ouch.

"It hurts!" I hissed, hardly able to find enough air through the pain to speak.

"Oh, *man!*" Daz said, his eyes widening. "Should I call 911?"

I looked back to Mom. If she thought I would be all right, then I knew I would be.

My heart skipped with fear when she frowned at him. "No, but I'm going to take Ana to the emergency room right away. I need you to stay here with Dad and help out, okay? Kevin, please go inside and ask the staff for some ice from the freezer." She turned back to me, gripping me gently on my shoulder. I blinked away tears as people from the party and zoo visitors started to notice us. They milled about aimlessly, trying not to stare. I could practically hear the confused thoughts.

There's that girl whose best friend ditched her.

She deserved it, I bet. For being such a liar.

I quaked under the pain, leaning back into my mother with a whimper. I didn't care that everyone could see me crying, because it felt like so much more than my wrist was hurting.

"It's okay. I think you've got a broken wrist. We'll get you fixed up, I promise." The way she looked deep into my eyes to reassure me made my throat tight. "Sit tight and try to think happy thoughts until we can get some painkillers into you."

Settling into her arms, I did my best not to cry anymore, but all of my happy thoughts seemed to skitter away on the wind like the dead leaves on the ground beside me. I'd wrecked my friendship. Wrecked my wrist.

And I'd only been thirteen for a few hours.

Chapter 16

When it is in danger, the short-horned lizard will make capillaries around its eyes explode, shooting predators with its own blood to startle them.

—*Animal Wisdom*

well, that's the world's strangest party trick right there.

Go figure that the *one* time I have to go to the hospital for something serious, it's on my bleeping birthday.

And of *course*, when I got there I looked like I'd been dragged through a pig pen, with tears streaming down my face and matted hair from my leap of idiocy from that bench in the zoo. And *yes,* everything with Liv seemed to crash onto me at exactly the same time as my wrist broke, so not only was I in actual bone-hurty pain, but I also had that horrible heart pain that even the best medication in the world can't fix.

To top it all off, I ended up getting the hot doctor at the emergency room. No way that I could get an old doctor with gray hair who looks like a grandpa, so I could feel somewhat *better* about myself.

No.

I had to get the guy that looked like a Ken doll, with perfect hair that lit up in an auburn wave under those horrible fluorescent lights.

And he smelled like peaches.

Are you surprised?

"A little bird told me that it's your thirteenth birthday," he said. He checked his chart. "Ana Jane Wright." He stretched out his hand to shake my non-broken one. I cringed at the movement, unable to find any words. So much more than my wrist felt broken.

"I'm Dr. Carriso," he introduced himself. "I'm going to make sure that you get out of here unscathed and back to normal, okay?"

I nodded glumly. *Normal* hasn't ever been my thing, but it wasn't worth mentioning. Especially since my version of normal would never be the same again with Liv so angry at me.

"We were at her birthday party," Mom said, giving me a sympathetic look. With everyone still at the party, Mom thought it would be best if Dad stayed and supervised with Grandpa, while the two of us came here. That meant I was not only missing hanging out with my friends, but also that I wouldn't get to blow out the candles on my own cake with everyone.

Dr. Carriso gave me a warm smile. "Not the best way to ring in your thirteenth year, is it? Mind if I take this off? We can't have you wearing any jewelry for the X-ray, I'm afraid. We can give it to your mom for safekeeping." He started to lift my sleeve, revealing the silver crocodile bracelet Ashley had given me. A grim thought rang out inside of me, telling me this was probably punishment for accepting it in the first place.

As he led me to the X-ray machine, a prickly fear swept over me. "Is this going to hurt?" I asked. For the first time, I thought about how the animals at Safe Haven felt, feeling hurt and wondering if they were going to be okay. It wasn't a nice feeling at all.

He shook his head. "Definitely not. You're a real trooper for handling the pain so well already. The X-ray takes a picture for us. It doesn't hurt at all. I promise."

I swallowed down my fear as he and Mom stepped

out of the room while the picture was taken. A few moments later, I was staring at the *inside* of my arm.

"Well, the good news is, everything is going to be perfectly all right," he said to Mom. His dimples were starting to remind me of Kevin. What would *Kevin* say about what had happened with Liv? I hadn't even gotten to spend any time with him at my party, and now he was probably already on his way to visit his brother.

"It's definitely broken." He turned to me.

"That's the good news?" I asked grimly. "What's the bad news then?" The realization fell over me like a damp, sticky spiderweb. I knew darn well what happened when you broke a limb. I was going to be like that little squirrel I saw at the center. Only not nearly as cute. "I'm going to have to wear a cast, aren't I?"

"I'm afraid so," he said. He began preparing the materials. "But don't be too scared. It doesn't hurt, and you only have to keep it on for six weeks."

I slumped against the hard white pillow on the examination bed. "Six *weeks*?! That's forever!"

Why did I jump over that stupid bench?!

"It will fly by," Mom cut in. "Think of how fast time has flown since you started school! It will be off before you know it!"

I knew she was doing her best to make me feel better, but all I could think was that I was going to be stuck with this eyesore of a cast for ages. Six weeks might as well be six *years*.

"And just think," Dr. Carriso said. "When you break a bone, it often grows back even *stronger* than it was."

I chewed on this as he began the process of casting my wrist. If bones grew back stronger when you broke them, what else did? Did *friendships* become stronger after they broke too?

When the cast was finished, I felt like I was dragging around an extra hundred pounds. I couldn't help but think about what Mr. Nicholson had said about influences, and how they can change how we act or what we do. I mean, if I hadn't chased after Liv, my wrist would have still been fine. But I *had* to, because things had gone so wrong. So my friendship with Liv actually influenced me to do something colossally dumb, like make a flying leap over that bench. But on the other hand (maybe one without a cast), if Liv had been normal, I wouldn't have felt like I had to hide the truth from her. All of the examples we talked about in class seemed to be all *good* influences. But what about bad ones? Can a good influence make a bad thing happen? It was all so confusing.

I watched as he secured the last section, wrapping the thick plaster covering around my thumb. A teensy feeling of relief buoyed me: at least it was my left hand, and not my writing hand or my doodling hand.

"When I was about your age, I broke my wrist too," Dr. Carriso said, washing his hands. "I was playing basketball." His nose crinkled. "Showing off, of course. But afterward, all my friends signed it and everything. Having a cast isn't so bad. It can be a walking reminder of all your friends, you know?"

I gave him a resigned smile as my heart clanged with thoughts of Liv. All the fight that had been in me when we'd arrived in the emergency room seemed to have drained out of me. Or maybe being in hospitals automatically makes you feel like crud. Maybe the air is too full of sickness for any good thoughts to make it through.

"Do you want to sign it?" I asked him, holding the cast out.

He grinned. "I'd be honored." He dug through his lab coat pocket and pulled out a green pen. "It's not every day I get to treat people on their very first day of being a teenager." He winked at Mom. "I promise, the rest of your teenage days won't be nearly so painful."

I sniffled as he leaned down to sign his name in sharp, artistic lines.

Proud to be the first friend to sign your cast! Take care, Ana!—Dr. C

"Thanks, Doc," I said, letting Mom help me drape my jacket over my shoulder. I didn't want to let him see the tears that had started pooling in my eyes again. All I could think was how, if nothing changed, Liv wouldn't be signing this cast at all.

By the time everyone was done spackling me with plaster at the hospital, the party had already been over for a few hours. The sun was dipping below the horizon, practically waving good-bye to my very first day as a teenager. And I'd spent hours of it in the emergency room.

But that didn't mean I'd missed everything. Dad and Daz had saved me a massive piece of cake. It was waiting for me with thirteen unlit candles stuck in it when we walked in the door.

"You can try all you want to avoid your mother's cake, kiddo," Dad joked, hoisting it toward me after I fumbled out of my jacket with my cast. "But even a broken wrist won't keep you safe!"

I did my best to smile as everyone crowded around me at the table. Grandpa and Sugar, who were chilling out in the living room when we walked in, both came up to give me an awkward-half-arm hug.

"Sorry about your arm, sweetie," Sugar said.

"That cast looks fab on you though!" she added. "Very adventurous and rustic!"

I grinned at her attempt to make me feel better. Of all the words to describe my new accessory, I don't think *adventurous* and *rustic* were the ones I'd choose.

Maybe *yutzy* and *embarrassing*.

"Thanks, guys," I said. "Did...did Liv say anything?" My throat was dry from the stale hospital air. "Before she left, I mean."

Dad squeezed my shoulder. "Sorry, we didn't actually see her leave," he said. "Once word got out that you were hurt, I made sure everyone was accounted for. Liv had already left. I called her mom, and she said she had picked her up outside the gates." He eyed Mom as I pictured Liv outside the zoo gates, ticked off at me and picking at the grass angrily.

Mom sucked in a breath. "Why don't you blow out your candles? I know the day hasn't exactly gone the way you wanted, but no daughter of mine is turning thirteen without making a birthday wish." I could tell by her cheery tone that she was trying to make the best of things and not let me tread down a nasty spiral of feeling sucky for myself.

I thought back to my last birthday wish moment. Technically, it had been my half birthday, and I was planning to wish that Liv could move home again.

She'd missed making the wish with me and even told me how much she *loves* living in New Zealand. Maybe that was when she started not wanting to be my best friend?

Taking a deep breath in, I focused on the purple-and-green frosted cake that Dad had placed in front of me. Thirteen candles flickered in my eyes, creating shadows and dancing lights on everyone's faces. I had to make this one count.

"I wish..." I took a deep breath and narrowed my eyes.

To find a way to be a good friend to everyone. Not just Liv. Not just Ashley. Everyone.

I blew out the candles in one try.

"Whoop!" Daz shouted. He was already starting to grab the melted candles, licking the icing off the bottoms. "Now we can feast!"

"Haven't you already had your cake, young man?" Mom shot him a bewildered look.

Daz shrugged. "Your first three slices of cake don't count," he said. "Everyone knows that."

Mom lifted her eyebrows as she swiped some icing from the side of his corner piece. "Tell that to my hips," she mumbled.

And I have to admit, despite the horrible day I had, everything *is* better with cake and gooey buttercream frosting.

Chapter 17

By wearing black fur with bright-white stripes, skunks warn other animals about their stinky spray. This is called aposematic coloring.

—*Animal Wisdom*

I wish that humans were able to show how dangerous they were by what they wore. Then we would know who to avoid, and we could also warn everyone else when we were in a bad mood!

Gossip is a lot like skunk spray. One minute it hasn't hit anyone yet, but the next, it's *everywhere*. I don't know how it happens. How one little incident can turn into something that's practically being read by the serious-sounding guy with the mustache on the nightly news.

The fact that I broke my wrist was all over school on Monday, and despite a bucketload of rumors, nobody seemed to know the truth. Even though a lot of people had been at my party, I guess Ashley hadn't told anyone *exactly* what had happened, but everyone seemed to think they knew.

Three Theories Why, I, Ana Wright, Have a Cast (In Order of Me Hearing Them on the Way from the Front Lawn of the School to Homeroom):

1. Eric (otherwise still known as The Guy Who Wears Too Much Cologne) told people that I was fighting a gorilla for a banana that ended up breaking my wrist in a *Planet of the Apes*–style fight. Odds of this are apparently four-to-one, according to the bets I heard.

2. Rachel from homeroom said that she heard that I was playing hopscotch, and a rogue buffalo charged me, stepping on my hand.

3. The weirdest theory came from Daz, who has been telling people that a crocodile bit my arm off, and that my cast is really hiding a cyborg arm now. He's even saying that I have a laser thing built in like Iron Man, which is probably the coolest part of his theory. The sad thing is, Daz was *there* and saw what actually happened,

but he's not giving up on his Iron Man theory for anything.

I'd only had a cast for one day, but I can tell you this already: casts definitely do *not* belong in junior high. So far, I'd already dropped my books twice, fumbled my lunch on to the floor (big sandwiches are hard to eat with only one hand), and accidentally closed my locker door on my thumb.

Now I have a weird bruise on my thumbnail that looks like a wombat.

The only bright side was now that people thought I was a gorilla-fighting-buffalo-outrunning-Iron Man-knockoff, they seemed a lot more scared of me, like I might suddenly whip out a cape and fly off out the window. That didn't get me out of schoolwork though. When Mr. Nicholson gave us a free period to work on our media projects, I knew I had to use every minute I could. The rest of my life was a ridiculous pile of zebra dung, but I couldn't botch this documentary too.

"Okay, guys." I herded Bella and Ashley out into the quiet hall, where Mr. Nicholson had said I could do some filming. "I need a few minutes with each of you, so I can film your spots for my documentary. I *need* to do well on this," I said, picturing that bright-red F on my quiz. With everything going wrong in my life, I deserved to win *something*, right?

"You're lucky I did my hair this morning," Ashley said, checking her reflection out with a pocket mirror. "Do we have to say anything special? Does the camera really add ten pounds?" She looked suspicious.

"You look beautiful!" Bella said, checking her own hair in Ashley's mirror. "All we have to do is answer Ana's prompts, like she said. Right?" She turned to me.

"That's it," I said, taking off the camera's lens cap with my good hand and shuffling Ashley against the wall where the light was nice and bright. "I'll ask you questions to prompt you about us, and then I'll edit it all together, and when I'm done, I'll have a wicked awesome documentary about everyone that influences me."

A dark thought crept over me as I spoke. Should I still include Liv in my film? I'd tried calling her a bunch of times last night but kept getting no answer. If I couldn't even reach her on the phone, how was I expected to film her? And was it right that *I* was the only one trying to fix us now? I mean, I knew I shouldn't have lied, but there were still lots of things Liv has done that she could have apologized for too. What about saying sorry for making fun of me with Leilani?

I sucked in a breath, forcing myself to get back to work. When the camera and lights were perfect, I gave Bella and Ashley a nod.

"'Kay, let's do this," Ashley said, squaring her shoulders.

I counted down, then turned the camera on. "So, Ashley," I started. "You and I never used to be friends, but I'm including you as one of my influences today because we hung out with sharks together in the summer and realized we don't actually hate each other. Can you talk a little more about that, and maybe about how we influence each other?"

Ashley cleared her throat. "Yep!" Her voice was bubbly and assertive, like I remembered from our summer presentations at the shark tank. "I used to *hate* Ana. Like super-duper hate."

I made a face behind the camera.

"But!" Ashley continued, fluffing her hair. "She dove in a shark tank to keep me from getting embarrassed. I mean, sure, it was *after* she pretty much tried to ruin my life, so it was all her own fault anyway. But, in the end, it all worked out, and I've actually learned a lot from her…"

I smiled, urging her to continue talking. She looked like she was on a real documentary!

"Like, I've learned that just because something is super geeky doesn't mean you have to pretend you don't like it. Ana likes a lot of crazy geeky things, but it's cool that she doesn't let other people make her feel dumb for it. And I think I've influenced her too.

Before she met me, she used to be shy, and I'm pretty sure that it's because of me that she found a backbone and stood up for herself." She winked at me.

"I mean, yeah. It was *technically* me she was standing up against, but you know. We both influence each other to be better people. I think. Wait, is that totally sappy?"

I grinned, hitting the stop button. That last line was perfect for the end of Ashley's segment. "That was awesome," I said, thanking her.

With Bella taking her place, I turned the camera on again.

"I'm Bella." She waved to me shyly. "And unlike Ashley, I've never really been afraid to be into geeky things." A small smile crossed her face as she peeked beside her, where Ashley was watching. "I've always loved museums and books and ancient maps and stuff. So I don't think that Ana influenced me in the same way that she did Ashley. But I do think that she helped me in another way."

I kept the camera steady, but my heart was beating fast. It was cool to learn that Bella was great at speaking on camera.

"Ana helped me learn that I could speak up," she said finally. She reached up to her hair, quickly tucking it behind her ear. "I don't have any brothers or sisters, but with Ana, it feels like I have a sister.

Same with Ashley. I feel like I have two sisters that taught me I can say what I'm feeling, and I don't have to keep it all hidden inside."

"Aw!" Ashley burst into the frame, wrapping her arms around her. "That's the nicest thing ever, you weirdo!"

Bella laughed as I struggled to hit the stop button without dropping them out of frame.

"That was *amazing*, guys!" I said, joining their hug. And yes, I couldn't speak for the two of them, but I definitely felt like a giant cheese ball for randomly hugging my friends in the hallway, but I couldn't help it. They were awesome. And now I had the footage to make the best documentary Mr. Nicholson had ever seen.

"Thank you so much," I said.

Ashley bit her lip. "Are you still planning on filming the sign at the zoo tonight?" she asked. Her eyes darted to Bella.

"Yeah," I said. "Why? You guys want to come?"

"Umm…" Ashley trailed off. Instantly she looked guiltier than a fox in a henhouse. "Maybe?" She raised her eyebrows to Bella. "What do you think, Bella? We can do that, right? Let's go hang out tonight at the zoo while Ana films…"

"Yes! Let's do that!" Bella said. Now *she* was the one who looked guilty.

"All right," I said, my shoulders slumping. "What is it? What are you two planning?"

"Nothing!" they both said in unison, with false-innocent smiles plastered onto their faces.

Say what you will about them, but they are *not* good liars.

When I showed up at the zoo after school to get a shot of the big sign out front for the opening sequence of my documentary, I couldn't stop peering behind me, looking for trouble. What were Ashley and Bella planning? Did it involve scaring the pants off me live on video?

But by the time I'd finished filming, they still hadn't shown up. It wasn't until I was packing up my camera that Ashley rushed up behind me.

"You're here!" She panted, bending over with her hands on her knees as she wheezed. "I thought we were going to miss you!"

Bella followed close behind her. Her short hair was whipped nearly straight up from the wind, giving her a girlie faux hawk.

I checked my watch. "Where have you guys been? I'm finishing up now."

Ashley shook her head, puffs of air clouding

around her face in the cold. "Nuh-huh." She gasped. "We were late—" She held up her shaking hand. Bella patted her on the back.

"We wanted to find you here," she explained. Her eyes were wide. "We asked Liv to come here."

I stepped back, feeling my heart flip-flop in my chest. "What?" I yelped. "Why? Why would you do that?! I haven't even been able to get her to respond to my texts." I gripped my camera bag right in my good hand, fumbling with my cast.

Ashley had regained her breath. "We went over to her hotel to talk to her and asked her to come here." She fingered through her wavy hair under her woolly hat, straightening out the static-fizzy pieces by her face.

"But *why*?!" I squeaked.

"Are you kidding?" she said. "You guys need an intervention, pronto."

I frowned. "An intervention? There's no way she's going to go for it! She hates me." The truth felt bitter in my mouth.

Bella grinned. "But she did go for it! I mean, she acted a little miffed about it all, but she's here! She's waiting for you in the Crocodile Pavilion right now! We've been rushing around all afternoon to make sure it's all lined up!"

My throat tightened. The fact that Ashley and

Bella had tried to do all this for me made my heart feel five sizes bigger in my chest.

"You did all that so I could talk to her?" I asked.

"We wanted to do something about it," Ashley said. "Obviously I don't *like* her, but she's your friend and all that. I know what it's like to have someone turn on you, no matter how hard you try to fix things."

My memory flickered to Rayna and how she had been giving Ashley the cold shoulder since she started hanging out more with me.

"I'm so sorry, guys," I said, scratching my cast nervously. "I lied to both of you, and I didn't mean to, and now you're doing this nice thing for me…"

Ashley moaned. "Apology accepted already! Now get *in* there and make up so all this work we did to convince her to come won't be for nothing! You're really annoying when you're all wigged out about her." She crossed her arms as Bella smirked.

"Okay," I said, gathering up as much courage as I could muster. I started to march toward the Crocodile Pavilion, a million thoughts buzzing through my head. "Wish me luck."

Chapter 18

A timber wolf can eat up to twenty pounds of
meat in a single sitting.

—*Animal Wisdom*

Daz can eat up to twenty pounds of Cool Ranch
Doritos in a single sitting too. The only time I
can eat that much is when I'm stress-eating. I
could go for some pie right now.

It was the first time in my life I was nervous to see
Liv. Instead of dealing with a thirteen-year-old girl
who used to love cardigans and musicals, I felt like
I was gearing up to face off against a deadly wild
animal. Kate's tips for handling wildlife were echo-
ing in my head.

No sudden movements.

Don't make eye contact.

Act swiftly and assertively.

When I saw her sitting on the bench in front of Louis's exhibit, I forced myself to smile.

"Hey," I said, giving her a tiny wave. She was decked out all in black again, with a patchwork backpack resting at her feet. She barely looked up to see me.

I sat down beside her on the bench. The air between us felt thick, despite the balmy breeze shuttering through the pavilion from the humidifier.

"Hey," she said. She shuffled away a couple of inches on the bench. She crossed her arms over her chest.

Not a good start.

But I wasn't going to give up yet.

"Thank you for coming," I said, trying to force my voice to sound normal. As upset as I was that Liv was mad at me, there was also a part of me that was super ticked at *her* for being so quick to hate me. Since when did friends not give each other a chance to explain? It was almost like she wanted our friendship over—the faster, the better.

I shoved the feeling down and continued. "I'm really sorry," I blurted. I nudged my camera bag under the bench nervously. I wanted to have a whole speech thought out, but the words were already streaming out of me like a waterfall.

"I didn't want you to find out I was friends with Ashley right away because things were so weird between us that first night. You weren't acting like yourself at all, and then things got worse and worse." I thought about my visit with Liv in her hotel room, with Leilani on video chat. Liv hadn't stood up for me at all. "But still. I'm sorry."

A weight that had seemed strapped to my chest started to dissolve instantly. No matter what happened now, at least I had apologized.

Liv sniffed, nodding once. "It was pretty crummy of you," she said. "I can't believe you're even friends with her," she spat.

I cringed. "I didn't want to hurt you. During the summer, Ashley and I got to hang out a lot at the marine exhibit. At first, *yes*, I thought she was out to sabotage me," I admitted. "But she turned out to be a pretty cool person. And a great friend." I thought about what she had said about us influencing each other for my documentary. Did Liv and I do the same?

"She helped get *you* here today, you know?" I added. "A lot has happened since you moved away. It's been hard. She's been one of the people who has actually helped me feel normal again."

Liv's lip started to curl. "I guess."

"Come on," I implored her. It wasn't fair that Liv was angry at me when she wasn't exactly the world's greatest friend this past week. "You're the one who's been acting all weird ever since you got here, and every time you turn around, you're texting with Leilani or—"

Liv interrupted me. "Leilani has nothing to do with this," she said icily.

I scoffed. "Doesn't she?! Ever since you got back, you've been like an entire different person! *I* wanted to keep things the same between us! *I* wanted to do something special to show you that you were still my best friend, no matter what. All this time I wanted to have you in a documentary about the people who influence me most in my life!" I was on a roll now, with heat building in my cheeks. There was so much I wanted to say to her.

"I tried so hard to show you that even though you were so *stinking* different, we could still be best friends! And yet, all you did every time we hung out was text with *Leilani*! You even asked her to video chat us that time! And then when she made fun of me, you laughed instead of standing up for me! What kind of a friend does that?! You couldn't *be* more different!"

Liv's jaw dropped. "*I'm* different?! Right!" she started, pointing her painted, navy-blue nail at me.

"When I moved away, you were like, the complete *opposite*, Ana! You were shy. You were quiet. You were *terrified* of Ashley. And now I come back for a stupid visit and suddenly you're not only besties with her, but you're some *star*." She made bunny quotes in the air and scrunched her nose like she was smelling something awful. "And you're standing in front of crowds yakking about animals and in stupid commercials acting like someone I don't even know! Oh, and let's not forget the random people coming up and asking for your stupid *autograph*!"

I shook my head, desperate to fight back, but she kept on yelling.

She turned the full force of her glare onto me. "Don't get me started about *changing*, Ana. You've changed more than I ever will! I'm just trying to keep up!"

My heart was pounding in my ears, but I couldn't let her believe that was true. "Is that what this is about? You're upset because I'm not some wallflower now, and I've changed *sooo* much?" I drew out the words sarcastically. "Your hair is *purple*! You used to be *nice* and now you're so snarky, with your stupid *dragon thing* in your ear. The Liv I know wouldn't laugh when someone made fun of me—she would tell them to shut up!" I struggled for the right words. "You've been changing for *months*!" I shouted.

Saying it out loud made me realize how true it was. You know how you sometimes don't notice a plant growing because you see it every day? But then, if you go away for a while, you come back and it's grown like three feet? That was what it seemed like with Liv. Her being away for so long made me realize how long she'd had to change in teensy, tiny ways. Then months later—*boom*—it seemed like she was instantly different. All this time, Liv had been slowly changing, away from me.

I didn't care that a few zoo stragglers were milling in and out of the pavilion. I didn't care that we probably looked like a couple of insane teenagers, fighting over some boy or something. All I cared about was that Liv *got* it.

"You come back with your purple hair and gigantic boots, and you're texting Leilani all the time, and 'Ohh, Leilani is so great, and *blah, blah, blah*,'" I imitated her. "You said you didn't even *want* to come visit now because of some stupid audition! Then the minute something goes *wrong* between us, you take off! You've been home for over a week and we've hardly hung out. You *left* my thirteenth birthday party! I'm never going to turn thirteen again!"

Liv sniffed. "It wasn't to *hurt* you. God! She was there when I was upset, okay?! More than I can say about *you*!" She wiped her eyes angrily with the sleeve of her black flannel jacket.

"Well, *good* for her," I said.

"And the reason I text Leilani a lot is because she's my *friend*!" she spat. "I didn't get to move and be surrounded by a whole bunch of people I already knew! I had to make all new friends, and she was someone who was nice to me from the start! Don't even get me started on *school*," she huffed, wiping her eyes.

I had no idea what she was talking about. "You love school! You're always going on and on about your drama classes and plays and being little miss social with Leilani! You tell me all the time!" I argued, throwing my hands up.

Liv rolled her eyes, scoffing. She seemed to be getting smaller and smaller, hunching over and holding her arms across her chest. "You know what, Ana? I don't need to sit here and listen to how sad you are that I've changed. You think you know everything about me and don't even care to know who I am *now*. I get that you're busy being this new Ana, being a celebrity and BFFs with Ashley," she said. "But this new Ana? I don't want to be friends with her."

My jaw dropped.

Had she seriously just said that?

My mouth stopped working, and it seemed like the angry thoughts in my head skidded to a halt. Every cell in my body seemed to sit up in shock.

For a moment, the silence took over. It seemed like the two of us might sit there forever, growing old and gray like people do in those time-lapse movies. Our hair could get stringy and white, and our skin could wrinkle up until we looked like two old prunes or those shrunken witchy heads that Daz had in his bedroom made from dehydrated apples.

Then she reached down, picked up her backpack, swung it over her shoulder in one swift move, and walked away.

She walked away.

My best friend in the whole world didn't want to be friends with me.

I turned to follow her, but something stopped me. I felt like if I stepped a foot away from that bench, that would make it all true. I would sit on that bench for days if it meant that I'd have my old friend back.

But she was already gone.

And judging by how angry she was, I had a feeling she'd been gone for a long time too.

Chapter 19

The badger is fossorial, which means it is adapted for digging and life underground. They often find prey by digging up their burrows.

—Animal Wisdom

If I had it my way, I would definitely want to disappear in a hole right now, badger style.

Sometimes bad things happen, and no matter how much you try to bury yourself with your blanket, the world isn't going to go away. At least that's what Mom said. The next day, I had my next session at Safe Haven.

Wrapping my scarf around my neck, I tucked

the ends into my coveralls and followed Kate deep into the woods where the cages were. It was hard to believe so little time had passed since my last visit to Safe Haven, especially since so much had happened. Best friendship meltdowns. Broken bones. And I was even a real *teenager* now.

Instead of feeling psyched and happy to be here, I felt like crawling in a hole and hibernating until springtime. Maybe bears had it all figured out. I had spent the night half starting text messages to Liv, only to end up deleting them. And she hadn't sent me any either.

"Ready to see your friend?" Kate asked, a glint of excitement in her eyes. She zipped up a thick, fleecy vest over her usual coveralls.

My spirits lifted a teensy notch. I was dying to see the fox that Mom had saved since my first day, but Kate had said earlier it would be best to wait for him to recover awhile longer. "Can I?" I asked. "I know Mom said that you were strict about people hanging around the animals unless it was absolutely necessary."

She nodded. "I'd say you earned your stripes—or should I say *spots*?—the last time you were here. I need to do a quick check on your fox today before the release. You can join in. We'll feed the squirrels while we're back there. You take the bucket of pellets and the water, and I'll grab the fruit."

Struggling with my cast, I used my fingertips to tug a mitten onto my good hand. I had figured school would be difficult to navigate with a cast, but I had totally underestimated how hard it would be to volunteer at the wildlife center with a bum hand. Already I felt like I was holding her up. Hoisting the food bucket up to my elbow, I rolled my eyes.

"Sorry," I mumbled to her as she waited for me to tug my other mitten over my bulky cast. "This thing doesn't do anything but get in the way." I gritted my teeth to hide my annoyance.

"Not a problem," she said, eyeing me carefully. "You're doing fine. I'm sorry that you got hurt on your birthday. Your mother called to let me know," she explained when I gave her a questioning look.

"The doctor said I had to keep it on for six weeks," I grumped. Following her down the path behind the clinic farther into the woods, I kicked a pebble with my boot. I felt a small blip of satisfaction when it ricocheted off a tree trunk with a sharp *thwack*.

When we reached the squirrel cages, I set the bucket of chow on the ground and began counting pellets. The cages were built deep in the woods, so the injured squirrels would be as close to nature as possible while they healed. The cages were bigger than I expected, taller than I was. Every day, Kate and the other volunteers made sure they had fresh water, new branches from nearby trees so they didn't get bored, and a handful of food.

"Each squirrel gets three pellets, right?" I asked, yanking off my mitten to count.

She nodded. "That's right," she said. "Cage A has four squirrels, B has three, and C has another four. So that's..." She trailed off, letting me do the math.

"Thirty-three pellets total." I scrunched up my nose.

Grinning, she gave me a thumbs-up, then went back to sticking a trail of fresh grapes through the bars onto the wooden struts. "Told you that you wouldn't need to take notes for everything." She winked. "The chow can be stuck in through the cages with the rest of the fruit, but you'll need to open the door to give them fresh water and stick in some new branches. I'll man the door so nobody escapes before they're ready."

I took a deep breath. The last thing I wanted right now was an escapee on my watch. Grabbing the strap of the heavy canteen, I slung it over my shoulder and started to unlock the latch of the door. Peeking in, I tried to locate each of the squirrels so they couldn't surprise me and escape. Their beady black eyes watched me intently, skittering close to where Kate had placed the grapes.

"Nobody freak out now," I begged them, stepping

in as fast as I could. My cast got caught on the door as I tried to shove it closed from the inside.

"Watch yourself," Kate said calmly. "You don't want to ruin all that lovely artwork."

I sighed, shaking my head. One thing I'd learned about having a cast is that *everyone* wanted to sign it. Kate might think all the signatures and messages from friends were "artwork," but right then I could have had an original Picasso painting on my cast and I'd still be annoyed.

With the door firmly shut, I changed the water while Kate hacked off some small branches from nearby trees.

When we were finished with the first cage, that familiar thrill ran through me again as I stepped out and relocked it. All those squirrels would be dead if it wasn't for us helping them, and soon they would be ready to be released again. The rest of the cages went faster, and soon we were heading farther into the woods, toward the large mammal enclosure.

"Now," Kate said, lowering her voice to a whisper. "We'll need to be extremely quiet. Foxes are incredibly skittish around people, and we want it to stay that way. She was looking quite out of sorts when she first arrived after your mother treated her, but I'm hoping she will be ready for release soon." She gestured to the large fence up ahead of us. "Here she is."

"Wait. It's a *girl*?" I gawked at Kate.

She winked. "Indeed she is. Sometimes animals surprise you!"

My heart skipped a beat as we approached closer. Willing my boots to step only on the quiet patches of dirt, I tiptoed to the fence. The enclosure was like a huge wire-fence box, with wooden corners keeping the whole thing intact. Inside, it looked like a giant woodland playground, with log beams, rocks, thick trees, and even a kiddie pool filled with half-frozen water.

And in the center of it all, curled up under a large, man-made rock cliff with her tail tucked around her snout, was my fox.

Okay, not *my* fox. But I couldn't help but feel a little protective of her, you know? I'd been there when she was stitched up, so that had to mean something. Her ears twitched in the breeze as we stepped closer. I couldn't help but wonder: Did she remember me like I remembered her?

A shiver zipped through me as she locked eyes with me. The rusty orange flickered like gemstones against her reddish fur. "She looks so much better!" I whispered.

Kate lifted her chin to peek through some of the trees in front of us. "Certainly has an appetite," she said. "That's good news." She pulled out her notebook and scribbled a few lines.

I gulped. Now that I was looking closer, I could see something small and furry on the rock in front of her.

Meat.

"Voles," Kate said, reading my mind.

I watched in awe as she stood, stretching her rump high in the air with her front paws digging into the ground. Her big, fluffy tail flicked at the air playfully. She lowered her head to chomp away on the meat at her feet. Her shiny, white canines were easy to spot, even from where we stood. And she was still wearing her blue bandage.

"Hey," I said, stifling my giggle. "We match." I held up my cast and waved it at Kate. "We both have hurt paws."

She nudged my shoulder playfully as we watched her eat. "Hopefully you're not as messy an eater as she is." She popped an almond from her pocket into her mouth and gave me a sly smile. "You know, this isn't the first time I've seen this particular fox."

I looked up at her. "It's not? Has she been hurt before?"

"Do you see that tiny orange tag fixed to her ear? It looks like a small earring." Kate leaned over, pointing through the fence.

I squinted. The tag was tiny, and against the orangey fur in her ears, it was easy to miss. "Is that an ID tag?" I asked. I'd heard that people sometimes tag animals to keep track of them in the wild.

"Indeed," Kate said, eating another almond. "She was here when she was a kit. Her mother had been hit by a car, and she and her two siblings were brought in. They were tagged then for some local researchers. Imagine my surprise when I examined her after she was dropped off last week!" she said, eyes twinkling.

"Whoa," I said, turning back to the fence. "So she's had a pretty tough life so far. Losing her mom, and then getting hurt again." A lump formed in my throat as I watched her. She was so beautiful, and I wished there were something I could do to go back in time so she still had her mom's help growing up.

Kate nodded. "She has. But most animals—most *everyone*—has challenges. I wouldn't have recognized her if it hadn't been for the tag," she said.

"Has she changed a lot? I mean, can you *tell* some animals are the same when you meet them again sometimes?" I took the almond that Kate was offering me. For some reason, pocket germs didn't seem so scary now.

Kate looked thoughtful. "Growing up can be tough, and it's no different if you're a wild animal with a big family like a fox or a tiny turtle that never gets to meet her parents. When she was here first as a wee thing, she was playful like all kits. Despite being in a rough state, she was open and curious. Now," Kate said, snuggling deeper into her scarf, "she's a lot more careful. And *much* more skittish. Life teaches some hard lessons. Foxes are very resilient though."

"That's good," I said. A warm feeling spread through my chest. Something about Kate's mellow Australian accent seemed to make me feel a little better.

"Sometimes, though," she continued, "I catch a glimpse of that little kit again." Her face broke into a wide smile. "Yesterday, she chased a bug through her pen, exactly like she did when she was a youngster! She may have changed growing up, but I think that little troublemaker is still in there!" Something about Kate's nostalgic eyes stuck in my mind. She gestured for me to look back at the fox, which was now chasing her tail like a dog. A *goofy* dog.

"Do you think I could come when she's released?" I asked Kate. Now more than ever, I knew I wanted to be there when he was set free. "I promise I won't get in the way."

Kate hoisted the food bucket back up over her shoulder. "I had a feeling you'd ask." She grinned sneakily. "I'm sure that can be arranged."

"And I was wondering…" I started, unsure of how to ask. "Would you mind if I filmed you working for a few minutes? It's for a project. *Hopefully* a project that will get me out of a bad grade." I grimaced.

Kate's eyebrows lifted curiously. "A project, hmm? On excellent fashion choices, no doubt." She brushed off her filthy coveralls playfully and struck a pose, fluffing her short, silver hair.

I laughed. "It's about the things that influenced us this year," I said, squirming against the cold. "I don't think I'd feel right if I didn't include you and this awesome place."

She pursed her lips as we turned around to head back to the clinic. "Ana, I would be honored," she said. Then, turning to me with that fierce glimmer in her eyes, she added, "But don't think that's going to get you out of skunk duty."

Chapter 20

Bald eagles will work together to hunt, with one animal scaring prey while the other snatches it up in its razor-sharp claws.

—Animal Wisdom

I wonder if bald eagles have BFFS.

Okay.

Voice-over segments? Check.

Footage of Bella, Ashley, Grandpa, Kate, and the zoo? Check.

Ridiculously giggly introduction featuring Daz? Check.

Music to make it all seem super professional? Check!

"You're almost done, Ana doll!" Sugar took a sip of her sparkling water and pointed to her laptop screen. Because I didn't have the right software to edit my documentary on my own laptop, Sugar had let me borrow hers. "You need to save the file on my desktop, then we can make a copy of it that you can take with you for your presentation. I'm so proud of you!" she squealed.

I clicked the mouse. So far, it had been fun going through all the footage with Sugar. She had helped me isolate the best parts featuring the zoo, my friends, and a hilarious scene of Grandpa singing and dancing to Frank Sinatra in the kitchen that he didn't even know I'd been there to film. Sugar had even shown me how to dub goofy music over that part. Since I wasn't sure that including Liv was a good idea, interviewing Kate meant that I had five influences. Technically, that meant my project was ready to go.

That didn't stop the clenched feeling in my chest, but every time I even thought about Liv, her words kept barreling through my head again at warp speed.

This new Ana? I don't want to be friends with her.

"What should I call it?" My right hand hovered over the keyboard. It was a pain to type with one hand, but I was already getting faster.

Sugar scrunched her nose and twirled a piece of

her hair with her finger. "How about Ana's A-Plus Project?" she asked. "It's smart to visualize what you want! Didn't you say you wanted to win an award with this?" Her eyes brightened. "I bet you have a great shot!"

My stomach tightened. "Don't remind me," I joked. The truth was, I couldn't wait for my chance to present. Almost everything about the past two weeks felt like one giant *stain* on my life, and that big, red F on my test seemed to magnify it all. Proof that I was failing in so many ways. Especially with my best friend.

No.

I shoved Liv from my mind again, focusing on what I *could* do. "I think I have a chance too," I said, feeling the hope grow inside me. "I don't know anyone else who did a documentary like this, and with your help, I think it turned out amazing." I lifted my drink up so we could clink glasses together. "Thank you!" I said.

"You're more than welcome! It's been so great getting to spend some more time with you!" She reached around and squeezed my shoulder, making sure to avoid knocking my super-awkward cast.

"How are we doing in here?" Mom peeked her head into my room. Darwin was perched on her shoulder, nuzzling her ear.

"We're good," I said as Sugar gave me a wink and went for a refill of her drink. "Project's done. I think I have a good shot at winning away my awful grade too," I added, hoping she would take that as a sign that I really *did* feel bad about it. Ever since I'd brought home that quiz for her to sign, I'd had about a million squinty-eyed, concerned looks from her.

She narrowed her eyes at me, then reached over to put her wrist against my forehead. Darwin crept down to her elbow and gave me his own suspicious look. "Are you okay? You look like a zombie," she said. "I know what happened with Liv has been awful, Ana. If you need to talk, I'm here, you know…" She turned the full force of her Mom-glare on me, picking away at my force field.

"*BRAACK!*" Darwin cawed. "Ana banana! *Zombie banana!*"

I ignored him. "I know, Mom. I just don't want to talk about it. I want to present my project and win. Are you guys going to come too?" I asked.

She beamed. "Of course we are! It's not every day your daughter stands in front of the world and—" She bit her lip, looking sheepish. "Well. You know. I guess it does happen from time to time, but I'm certainly not missing out on hearing what my daughter has to say. It should be fun!"

I rolled my eyes.

Honestly, Mom had a weird sense of "fun."

"Are you all ready to go then?" Her eyes drifted to my laptop screen, where the names of my five influences were floating in a bubble of text on my opening sequence. I knew by her face that she was surprised to see that Liv wasn't on the list, but she didn't say anything.

"All done," I said, closing my laptop.

"Well then," she said, looking pleased. "Let's go have some fun that *doesn't* involve school projects, huh?" She winked, wrapping an arm around me. "We've got a fox to set free!"

My heart leaped. "Right now?!"

She started for the door. "Kate just called! Let's get a move on, Fox Whisperer!"

The forest seemed to grow thicker around us as Kate and Mom hoisted the metal cage from the back of the truck. A gray blanket was covering it, so the fox probably had no idea where she was. I hoped with all my heart that she'd be happily surprised when they opened that door.

Safe inside the truck, I was practically glued to the window. I wanted to be outside with Kate, but Mom made short work of that.

"How do you know she's going to be okay?" I asked nervously. For some reason, I wasn't as excited as I thought I would be, knowing she was on her way home again. Even though she was completely healthy now, I still felt a strange sense of unease knowing she was going back into the dangerous wilderness. She'd already been at the wildlife center twice in her short life. What if she got hurt again? "Maybe we should keep her in the zoo, so we *know* she'll be safe."

Mom sighed. "We don't know," she said, smiling gently. "But she's a healthy, beautiful animal and deserves to be free. She isn't an animal that needs the zoo." She tucked a strand of messy hair behind her ear. "We've done what we can to help her recover. But sometimes, you can't save everything. All you can do is your best, and then you have to let go."

Her words seemed to hang in the air of the quiet forest. *All you can do is your best, and then you have to let go.*

It sounded almost like a poem.

"Why can't I be out there?" I asked. I wanted more than anything to be outside with Kate, like a *real* wildlife rehabilitator, setting the fox free. "I won't do anything wrong, I promise. And I'll be super careful. She won't hurt me!"

Mom frowned. "No, she wouldn't *mean* to hurt

you. But even animals that seem perfectly gentle can act quite vicious when they're cornered."

Something stirred inside me. "What do you mean?" I asked. My cheeks started to burn, even though the heat inside the truck had long since disappeared.

"When they're threatened—or when they feel like their way of life is in danger—some animals can lash out. They can hurt you, but they're only trying to defend themselves. It's a way of protecting themselves when they're scared."

My stomach bottomed out. I was staring out at the trees, but nothing was in focus. Suddenly, I blinked, and it felt like I was looking at the forest with new eyes. The puzzle in my head finally clicked into place. All I could think was, *that's exactly what happened with Liv.*

My mind raced, pulling together all the details from every time I'd seen Liv. All of her snippy talk about me being a "celebrity." Being weird and moody while I had to sign that autograph. Flipping out and being so angry when she saw me hanging out with Ashley. She wasn't only sad that I was different.

She was *threatened* by it. *Scared.*

Just like I was scared that *she* was changing so much.

Only instead of handling it like I did (which, let's face it, was super confused and full of lying), she lashed out at me. She was so scared she even made fun of me with Leilani, probably because she didn't want to mess things up with the only friend she had at home. I'd practically done the same thing with Ashley when I'd lied about Liv knowing we were friends now.

I swallowed hard, seeing the past two weeks for what they really were: two friends who were different and scared of messing everything up, both with their new friends and their old ones. It wasn't nice, and it wasn't on purpose, and like Kate had said about our fox, I could still see glimpses of the old Liv behind all the new parts that were lashing out.

For the first time since she'd arrived here, I could actually *understand* Liv. The truth seemed to expand in my head like a balloon, crushing out all the annoyed and hurt thoughts from before.

I leaned back in my seat, suddenly feeling light-headed. But Kate was still moving outside, getting into position.

I nestled closer to Mom as I watched Kate tuck herself behind the cage they'd placed in the thicket. She checked that we were safely in the truck, then with one swift movement, yanked on the cable that connected to the cage door. I watched in awe as the wind in the trees seemed to slow to a stop, waiting for the fox to make her way from the cage. Kate held her hands over her chest, like she was bracing herself.

"You're free!" I whispered. Mom grabbed my hand, squeezing it tightly.

At first, there was nothing. No movement from inside the cage. No movement from Kate. Beside me, Mom held her breath.

Then a paw appeared.

She looked so scared.

Mom's hand tightened again around mine as the fox crept from the cage, with its head down and its shoulders slinking left to right slowly. Carefully. She seemed so much larger now, so much more *wild*. My breath caught in my chest as the last of her long, black tail appeared through the cage door.

"Good luck," I whispered again, leaning closer to the window. I placed my hand on the cold window, wishing I could give her one last pet.

The fox didn't seem to realize anything was strange about this moment—with the three of us gawking at her. Before lifting her paw to step again, she turned to face the truck.

Her eyes locked with mine, sending a thrill deep into my stomach. They were rusty brown, like they'd been that night at the hospital. But this time, they were much brighter.

She would survive. I knew it.

I closed my eyes, wishing her a long and happy life in the forest.

And then she was gone.

Kate lifted her fist in victory as the fox's tail disappeared into the bushes, her reddish-orange coat already fading against the tree trunks.

"I think she'll be fine," Mom said, resting back against her seat with a sigh. Soft snow had started to fall around us.

"It's snowing for her," I pointed out. Unrolling my window, I stuck my mitten out, catching the first crystal snowflakes. Touching one to my tongue, I smiled. "I think she's going to be better than fine."

And maybe it was the way the whole world seemed to turn into a giant snow globe for us, but I felt like the weight from my shoulders had disappeared. I'd get a shot to fix my botched grade tomorrow, and even Kevin was coming home.

"Time for burgers to celebrate?" Mom asked, licking her lips.

I nodded, taking one last look out the window. "Better than voles," I said, waving out the window.

I knew my fox was already far away, but I had a feeling she could tell I was saying good-bye anyway.

"Can we make a quick stop a home first?" I asked as Mom started the engine.

"What could possibly be more important than burgers right now?" she asked, grinning.

"My project," I said. "I need to make one quick change."

For the first time in weeks, I knew exactly what to do.

Liv,

I know you're mad at me. And yeah, I'm mad at you too. We both did some awful stuff. But I have something I want you to see. I hope you can come to the school tomorrow night for our projects. I'll be presenting around 7:30.

—Ana

Chapter 21

A chipmunk's heart beats about three hundred and fifty times per minute. When they hibernate, their heart rate drops to only fifteen times per minute.

—*Animal Wisdom*

Know what else can make your heart race? Trying to talk your way out of a big fat F!

"I'm freaking out," Brooke said. "I'm totally and completely freaking out. I can't *do* this!"

I nearly dropped my laptop when I heard Brooke's shrill voice down the hall. It was the night of our media presentations, and so far, I'd managed to not make a complete zebra-butt out of myself.

But, of course, the night was still young.

As Mom and Dad wandered through looking at the projects with the rest of the teachers and parents, I checked my video one final time. Like Mr. Nicholson had asked, I had a speech prepared for each influence I'd be including, and I was ready for my big moment to wipe my F record clean. I also made sure that the new segment looked perfect.

I was also on the lookout for Liv.

After the fox release yesterday, I knew I had to include her in my documentary. Like Grandpa said, documentaries are supposed to represent *reality*, not some sugary, fake version of the life you wish you had. And Liv was one of the biggest influences I had. She didn't help me be braver, like Ashley. And she didn't help me own my weirdness, like Bella. Liv influenced me to be *real*, to face the truth and fight for the things that mattered to me.

Even if it hurt.

But more importantly, I felt for the first time that I knew where Liv was coming from. She was like that fox, and by lying to her about Ashley along with all the other big changes about my life, she'd felt threatened and lashed out.

I *knew* it was true.

Now I just needed her to know it too. Maybe then we would have a chance.

Last night, after going through all my old photos of us together, I was able to put together a supercool video collage of the two of us to include. Holding hands as we crossed the street as tiny kids, goofing off with ridiculous pigtail braids in second grade, and even our horribly awkward "make our own clothes" phase, where we looked like orphans from a bad musical.

It was all set, and I was certain that I'd win my way to a better grade with it too.

"I'm going to *puke*!" Brooke's voice hissed through the hall again. "There are too many people here! I can't do it." She was practically hyperventilating now. Beside her, Ashley and Bella were trying to calm her, but it was obvious by the nervous looks in their eyes that they weren't getting anywhere with her.

Frowning, I clicked my video into ready position and made my way over. The memory of her at my very first crocodile presentation flickered back to my mind and how she'd tried to help me stay focused, no matter how many people wanted to me mess up. She had helped save my butt once, and now was the chance to do the same for her.

"Brooke," I said, grabbing her arm and trying to use my best soothing voice. "You need to stop freaking out! You're going to be okay."

"See!" Ashley blurted, shooting me a grateful look. "It's all going to be perfect! I mean, you don't *need* to win the grade thing," she said. "All you need to do is avoid barfing all over a teacher and you're golden!"

I gave Ashley a look, while Bella hid her giggle.

Brooke wrung her hands together as she spoke. "There are too many parents here. And all these *teachers*. Why did I pick a medium that used hardly any words?! Now I'll have to *say* everything!"

I shook my head. "Remember what you told me during the summer? When Ashley wanted me to botch up my croc presentation?" I tapped my forehead with my finger. "Focus! All you have to do is forget about everybody watching you and focus on the words you need to say. You're allowed to read from your paper! Just focus on these words." I held up her paper.

Brooke took a breath, slower this time. "Focus. Fine," she sputtered. She wasn't looking normal yet, but she was on her way. "You guys won't make fun of me, right?" she asked suddenly. "If I completely mess up?"

Ashley rolled her eyes. "We're *all* going to mess up, Brooke," she said matter-of-factly. "Join the club."

That seemed to shake the last of Brooke's fears away. As I made my way back to my table, I took one last look around. Still no Liv. Now it was my turn to start worrying. Could she be so upset that she wouldn't show up, despite my note? Had she changed that much?

Then a familiar hand waved in the air.

"Ana!" A voice carried over the noise of the hallway. But it wasn't Liv.

It was her *mother*.

"Mrs. Reed!" I yelled, waving her over. My heart skipped as she hurried over. Her face was pale. Mr. Reed followed close behind, with my parents tailing him. Mom and Dad must have seen them come in.

"What's wrong?" I asked, my stomach clenching.

"Have you seen Liv?" she asked, gripping my hands. "She told me that she would be here. Is she with you? Have you seen her?"

My stomach flip-flopped at the concern in their eyes. For a moment, I wanted to cover for Liv because that's what friends did. Maybe she was out for a bit and told her parents we'd be together so they'd let her go?

But, if that was the case, wouldn't she have told me? Maybe she was hurt?

"She's not with me," I said, hating the rush of disappointment inside myself. "I'm sorry. I actually asked her to be here tonight so she could see my presentation. But she didn't show up. She didn't even text me."

She really didn't want to be my friend now. The truth felt like a cold, wet blanket, weighing down my shoulders.

Mrs. Reed's face tightened as Mom grabbed her arm. "Don't worry, Leah," she said. "We'll find her. I'm sure she stepped out of the hotel for some air. You know how upset the girls have been…"

I closed my eyes, trying to ignore the noise around me. When Liv and I were little, we used to try to read each other's minds, standing at opposite ends of the room, thinking of certain colors or animals. One time, we got eight out of ten right.

I squished my eyes shut tight, trying to tune in to her now. It could work, right?

Where are you, Liv?

The image of a cherry shake bubbled up in my mind. A lot may have changed between us, but the Liv I knew would never stop loving ice cream when she was upset.

"That's it!" I said, jerking my head up. "She's at Shaken, I know it. It's where we always used to go when we were sad. She *has* to be there."

Before I could say anything else, Mrs. Reed thanked me and bolted for the doors in a rush, with my parents following. "We're so sorry to miss your presentation, hun," Mom called back. "We'll be back once we know for sure that Liv is safe and sound, okay?"

I shifted on my feet as Mr. Nicholson began clapping his hands to get everyone's attention. Students straightened up, rushing back to their tables so they would be ready to present. Everyone wanted to win that free pass to drop their worst grade, and the halls were already buzzing with excitement. I knew that if I stayed, I could win this thing.

But I also knew there was no way I was staying.

I didn't know if Liv was okay right now, and there was no way some stupid grade was going to stop me from making sure.

"I'm coming with you!" I said to Mom, taking off after her.

She whirled around, looking sympathetic. "No, Ana! I promise you, we're going to go there and pick up Liv. You need to worry about your project right now. This is your only shot at that pass!"

"My grade doesn't matter. I'll feel a lot worse if I fail at this, you know?" I gave her a pleading look.

She stared at me for a second, then nodded. "Let's go."

Liv might not have wanted to be my friend right then.

But that didn't mean I couldn't be hers.

Chapter 22

Raccoons appear to "wash" their food with their hands before eating it. In fact, they are using their sensitive paws to identify what they are eating.

—Animal Wisdom

If raccoons have sensitive paws, do they also have sensitive hearts? Can raccoons get worried about their friends? I think they can.

The bright-red sign at Shaken, Not Stirred flickered against the inky backdrop of the night sky. As Mr. and Mrs. Reed hopped out of their car, I urged Dad to park faster.

"Come on!" I said, unbuckling my belt. "Can you see her? Is she in there?"

Mom craned her neck to see inside. "I can't tell." Rushing for the front door, we all followed after the Reeds, like a clamoring conga line of elephants in snow boots.

And there, in a booth against the turquoise-blue wall, was Liv.

In *our* booth.

Relief surged through me as I practically skipped over to her, following after Mrs. Reed.

"Olivia Peyton Reed!" she started. Her hands whipped over her chest as she gawked at Liv. I lurched to a stop, holding myself back. I hadn't expected Mrs. Reed to be so upset with Liv, but if I was honest with myself, even *I* was mad at Liv for giving us all such a scare.

"Are you all right?! Do you have any idea the *worry* you've caused tonight?! First sneaking out at home, and now this?! You scared us half to death!"

Wait, *what*? I caught Mom's eye, but she didn't react.

Sneaking out at home? *Huh?*

I expected Liv to immediately apologize or to say that she'd been upset or *anything* to show she hadn't meant to cause such a stir. But instead, she stared straight ahead at her mom. She looked so angry.

"I just wanted a shake," she said quietly. She gripped the straw with her purple mittens.

It was Mr. Reed's turn to be upset. "Liv, you can't just go running off like this! It isn't safe! We wouldn't have even known where you were if it weren't for Ana." He pointed at me, causing my face to heat up. I wasn't sure if I wanted Liv's anger focused on me right now either. "Thank heavens she was right!" he added.

Liv glared at me. "Of course she ratted on me," she said simply.

A cold fist gripped my insides. "I didn't rat on you!" I shouted. "I was worried about you! I made this awesome presentation that *included you*, even though you said you didn't even want to be friends! How is that ratting on you?! And I actually missed my chance to present because of this!" I clenched my fingernails into my palms.

For a moment, her angry face faltered. And just like that, I caught a glimpse of what Liv was feeling.

Not only sad. *Threatened.* It was easier to spot it now that I knew the truth. Her mouth quivered slightly.

Mrs. Reed sighed, then sat down at the booth across from Liv. She hung her head, looking defeated. "Ever since we moved, we've had some school issues," she said to my parents. "Her grades

are slipping. She's skipping classes. Her attitude...
Well." She turned to Liv. "The girls at school... I
know this behavior might seem to work for them,
but I promise you, it is *not* going to work for you."
Mrs. Reed's voice was low, but her eyes were gentle.

Another puzzle piece clicked in my head. Like
Ashley and Bella influenced me at school, I bet
Leilani had influenced Liv.

And by the sounds of it, it wasn't in a good way.
Skipping school?

Liv's mouth squished together into a thin line.
"Do we need to talk about this now, *Mother*?"

I couldn't believe she used that tone, and I nearly
stepped back to get away from Mrs. Reed's response.

"Yes," Mrs. Reed said firmly. "We do. I think
you owe these people an explanation as to why
they had to take time away from their busy night
to track you down."

Liv's shoulders slumped. "I'm sorry," she said,
looking from Mom and Dad to me. "I really am."

"We'll talk about this more at the hotel," Mrs.
Reed said, rubbing her temples. "Jane, Henry." She
smiled sadly at my parents. "I'm so sorry to ruin
your night."

My parents made a show of how it was no big
deal and started out the door.

"Wait," Liv piped up. "Can I talk to Ana for a

second? Before we go?" She looked at Mrs. Reed. The apology was clear in her eyes.

Mrs. Reed took a deep breath. "You've got five minutes," she said gently, then filed out the door after my parents.

"Hey," I said, sliding into the booth across from Liv. I couldn't help but feel bad for her.

She sniffed, and I could instantly tell she was trying to put on a brave face.

"Listen," she said. "I'm sorry about what happened. I wanted to go tonight. Then I got there and saw you talking with Ashley and Bella in the hall and..." She grimaced. "It sucks to see you being so happy now without me. It's almost like you're *happier* I'm gone, you know? And when I saw how great you were doing, I wanted to make it seem like *I'm* that great too, but the truth is my classes are super hard and I've been at the principal's office three times this year. It's been really weird figuring it all out, you know?" She shook her head.

I didn't know what to say to that, but I kept looking at Liv so she knew I was listening. It was hard to imagine Liv being sent to the principal's office if it wasn't as a classroom helper or something.

She sighed. "I'm sorry. And not only for tonight, which...*sucked*." She gestured out the door where our parents were starting their cars. "But every-thing. I know I can be a jerk when—"

"You were scared," I interrupted.

Liv blinked in surprise. "I...I was. Really scared."

"I know," I said. "Me too. I think I just handled it differently. I tried to lie. I tried to hide all the changes between us or hope that they weren't true."

"I mean, I think what you did was super crummy." I kept talking. It was easier to say the words than I thought it would be, and the minute they were out of my mouth, the pit in my stomach disappeared. I hated making Liv feel bad, and I especially hated that she was going to get on a plane soon and I wouldn't see her for ages again. But that was why I had to tell her the truth. She deserved it.

"You're my best friend," I said, weighing my words one last time. Just like with my fox, I had to let it go and see if our friendship could survive. One more time. "But since you've been back, you've been *terrible* at it!"

Liv's eyes widened, and she blinked in surprise. "Terrible?" She sniffled.

I couldn't help but giggle at how pathetic we must look, but thankfully the shop was empty, except for the waitress in the back room.

"Terrible," I said.

She nodded. "I don't know *how* to be friends like

we were before," she admitted, lifting her shake to take a sip through the straw. "I mean, I don't feel the same as I did a year ago, you know? But it seemed like all you wanted was for me to be like I used to be."

"It *was* what I wanted," I admitted. "But I'm not the same either, like you said. I think we've both changed a lot."

"Right," she said, dabbing her eyes. "So I don't know how we can be best friends like we were anymore. I mean, I *want* to! We were so super close! But we aren't little kids now. We're too different. You *are* practically a celebrity. And I'm going to have friends that you don't like. And we're only going to get *more* different as we get old." She huffed, crossing her arms.

I smiled, trying to keep Leilani out of my thoughts. "But different isn't *bad*. Maybe we don't *need* to be like that anymore." I reached over to take a sip of her shake. The taste of cherries made me shiver. My next words were painful coming out, but I knew they felt right. "Maybe we don't even need to be 'best friends' at all, because who cares about that anyway?"

I thought of Liv and Bella and Ashley, who were all so different, yet all great friends to me. Were any of them truly *best*? Because to me, I sort of felt like I needed all of them. Ashley was gutsy. Bella was sweet. Liv was a giant purple-haired goofball that I'd known forever, who secretly loved math and apparently was friends with some pretty shady girls now. "Maybe we can be *real* friends, without all the stuff that made us so crazy, like trying to *be* a certain way."

Her frown tipped up. "I think you're right," she said softly. "It seems like you've been trying to be you, and *I've* been trying to make you understand that I'm not the same. We both…" She trailed off.

"Collided," we said in unison.

"*Jinx!*" we yelped, laughing.

"Best friends seems so *ancient*, you know?" she continued, sighing heavily. "Like we're fossils, who will never change again. I think it's because we've called ourselves that for years now, back when we *were* the same for a long time. I want to stay friends and still be able to change however we want without worrying you're going to ditch me because we're *not* exactly the way we used to be."

"*Real* friends then," I said, sitting taller. "Real friends can change and dye their hair and become gigantic nerds who work in the zoo and smell like skunk half the time and have other friends. And no matter what, we'll be there for each other. Who needs a best friend when you can have a real one, right?" I smirked. "Best friends is *so* last year," I said, borrowing half a phrase from Ashley. "Let's be real friends and see who we become."

A gentle quiet passed between us. Part of me was scared to stop being *best* friends with Liv, like I was carving a hole out of my life. But now, like digging a hole in a garden, maybe something new and better would grow there. The ambient noise of the ice-cream machines seemed louder than it had a second earlier.

But this time, it wasn't awkward. Just silence.

Liv smiled. "Deal," she said, narrowing her eyes.

My heart blipped with nerves as I saw the serious look on her face. "What is it?"

"One more thing," she said. Curiosity prickled inside me as she dug through her patchwork backpack, searching for something. She dug around in her bag, then waved a green pen in front of me, her eyes glinting with gleeful excitement.

"I need to sign that cast of yours!" she said, yanking my arm closer. "Everyone else got all the good spots!"

As I watched her sign, it hit me that soon, Liv and her parents would be up in the air again, winging their way back home to New Zealand. And I would be here again, without her. But as much as her visit had messed us up, I kind of felt like we were maybe better for it, you know? Like Dr. Carriso had said, maybe our break would make us grow back even stronger.

He was a *doctor*, after all.

"Wait," Liv said as we headed for the door. "Your presentation! You can still do it! Go and get that free grade! Mom, can we go back so Ana can do her presentation?"

Mrs. Reed shivered in the cold. "It's seven thirty on a Friday night. Where *else* would we be? I think Ana deserves it after what's happened tonight!" She winked.

Chapter 23

Despite their name, black bears aren't always black. They can also be brown, blond, blue gray, cinnamon, or white.

—Animal Wisdom

Cinnamon bears?! That sounds like the cutest thing ever!

I dashed down past the lockers to the main hall, searching for Mr. Nicholson. But when I turned a corner and saw him in the middle of the crowd, he was already holding up Bella's hand.

"Ladies and gentlemen, I'm happy to announce our winner is Bella Rodriguez, for her wonderful presentation using antique hardcover books!"

My heart sank. "I missed it," I said, shaking my head. Liv crossed her arms beside me, looking like she wanted to start a riot.

"Well, that isn't fair!" she started. "I'm going to go over there and make sure that—"

"No, Liv!" I pulled her back. "Bella won. That's pretty fantastic actually! Don't mess this up for her." I gave Bella the teensiest wave when I caught her eye, followed by a geeky thumbs-up. Ashley and Brooke were right beside her, cheering her on as Mr. Nicholson handed her the "official" slip, getting her out of her chosen grade.

"Argh, *fine*," Liv said. "I'm sorry you lost out because of me. I'm sure you would have crushed it."

I shrugged. "I'll have to convince Mr. Nicholson to let me present to him later," I said. A small niggle of doubt crept up in me. Mr. Nicholson could be super strict on project deadlines, but I was sure he'd give me a chance once he heard my excuse.

"Maybe I'll have to throw in some extra credit," I said, uncertain. "Hey," I said, poking Mom in the shoulder. "I have to go to the bathroom, okay? Too much cherry shake."

Shouldering my way through the crowd into the bathroom, I turned the faucet on full blast. I didn't need to pee. I just wanted a minute alone. The rush of water drowned out the noise outside. Suddenly, now that I was alone, the weight of the evening seemed to crash down on me.

Missing out on my project.

Finding Liv after that horrible scare.

Cherry shakes and casts.

So much had happened and it seemed like every emotion was lining up inside of me, demanding its turn. I guess this is why they say that being a teenager is so hard—half the time it seems like your feelings can't even fit in your body anymore.

Staring at my blotchy face, I leaned my head against the mirror.

"Ana?" A timid voice echoed against the concrete, beige walls. "You okay?"

I sniffed, wiping my eyes. I hadn't realized I had tears in my eyes.

"I'm fine," I said, cringing at how hoarse my voice was.

Kevin appeared in the doorway.

"Kev!" I surprised myself with how happy I sounded. "What are you doing here?! I thought you weren't back until tomorrow! You can't be in here!"

Flushing with embarrassment, I turned the faucet off and yanked a few yards of paper towel from the machine. I dabbed my eyes, trying not to smear whatever sad goop was in them all over my face. I was too strung out to go up and hug him like a normal person who hadn't seen her boyfriend in days.

He frowned. "We got home early, and I thought it would be nice to see you. Are you crying?" he asked. My heart clenched with happiness. Life wasn't *right* without Kevin, I realized. Like a fox without teeth or an ice-cream shake without the cherries. Kevin helped to keep me *sane*.

"I didn't think I was," I said, exhausted.

"That's not the face of someone who won back a free grade," he said. "What happened?"

"I missed it," I said simply, throwing up my hands. "We all thought Liv might be in trouble, so we had to go to Shaken, Not Stirred to find her, and thank God she was there, but by the time we talked it all out and started to feel a little bit better, it was too late for me to come back here and present my documentary, even though I *really* wanted a shot at that free pass, because I hate the thought of some giant *fail* on my report card, and it was such a good project, but now there's nothing I can do about it, so I'm in the bathroom, then I randomly started crying because…because, I don't know. Liv is going back soon, and we're *friends*, but this past week has been…*ugh*." My voice ran out of breath at the end of my rant, leaving me wheezing.

His eyes softened. "You found Liv though?"

I nodded glumly as he came over to give me a hug. Sniffling into his shoulder, I probably got mucky tears and goobers all over him. But Kev didn't move. He did reach for a tissue for me though, so obviously I was a complete phlegm monster.

"Thirteen sucks," I said. "Every time I think I have something figured out, it's like the whole world flips upside down again and I'm stuck trying to juggle in zero gravity."

Kev nodded appreciatively. "Nice one!" He beamed. "Maybe you *have* missed me. What do you want to do about your project?"

I hung my head lower, scratching under my cast the best I could. "There's nothing *to* do. I know Mr. Nicholson will hear me out, and he'll let me present it to him. But you know what he's like about late stuff and his policy on docking grades. I kind of feel like I need something *extra* now to make up for ditching. It was *so* good, you know?"

"You could give him a two-part project," he suggested. "Even though you won't win the free pass, I bet you won't lose points for it."

I looked up at him. "What, like tonight? There's no way!"

The dimple appeared on his cheek. "That doesn't sound like the Ana I know," he teased.

I grinned for the first time in what felt like ages.

"What? Am I supposed to magically create something razzle-dazzly to distract him from the fact I wasn't even there tonight?"

He nodded. "That's one idea, for sure." He took my hand, lacing his fingers awkwardly through my ragged cast. "But there's got to be something else. Something that will go perfectly with your documentary."

I let my eyes nearly droop closed as I watched Kevin's fingers slowly drumming on my cast. Dr. Carriso's loopy writing stared back at me.

"Proud to be the first friend to sign your cast!"

Then something hit me. And this time it wasn't how much being thirteen felt like being stuck in a giant vat of monkey poop. I didn't need to make another project. I already had the perfect addition to my documentary.

"Kev," I said, pulling myself taller, "you're a *genius*!"

His eyes lit up with surprise. "I am?"

I beamed at him. For a moment, it crossed my mind that we were in the girls' bathroom, and this probably wasn't the most romantic spot in the world. But Kev's idea—or maybe it was *my* idea that he helped me find—swept over me with such an impact, I couldn't help myself.

I kissed him.

Yes!

I know!

I was snotty faced with a cast on my wrist, and the girls' bathroom wasn't the most exciting first kiss story, but it was now *my* first kiss story, because I downright planted one on Kevin without even thinking.

After all this time, wondering, hoping, planning, *wishing* for this moment, I couldn't believe how fast my lips were able to find his. I didn't think about *how* to kiss him or where I should lean my head or how to avoid giving him a nosebleed (like last time—no need to replay that little trauma bomb) or what my breath smelled like or whether or not my eyes were red and my nose was runny or even about kiss pacts.

Instead, I was just kissing him.

And you know what?

It.

Was.

Awesome.

"Whoa," Kev said when I pulled away. If there's one thing I know now about kissing is that while you're *in* the moment, you can feel totally cool and not embarrassed at all. But the minute you *leave* that moment, it becomes Awkward City all over again. What's up with that?

"Um…" I blinked at him, half enjoying the dazed look on his face and half-terrified that I looked as goofy as he did. Considering the swirly-whirly butterflies in my stomach, my odds were not looking good.

"Sorry," I said.

"No!" he said, shaking his head. "Don't apologize for that. That was…"

I grinned at him, probably looking like a full-on psychotic person.

"Right?!" I giggled, then commanded myself to pull my goofball self back together. "I wanted to thank you. For helping me come up with the perfect idea."

He tilted his head. "What's your big idea then?"

I rubbed my hands together like a scheming housefly. "I'll tell you once we get out of here. Sorry our first kiss was in the girls' bathroom," I added, standing up. "I mean, of all the places where I'd imagined our first kiss happening—not that I was just sitting around *imagining* it because that would be a little crazy—but, um. You know." I was babbling now, and the feeling was returning to my toes again. "I just think it's kind of funny, you being in here…" I giggled.

"Uh…Ana?" Kevin said, holding the door open for us to leave.

"Yuh-huh?" Clearly I was still in a daze over our kiss, no matter how über-chill I was trying to be.

He pointed at the sign on the door, where the little stick man *without* a skirt on was staring back at me.

Wait.

"Yep." Kevin grinned, taking my hand. "This is the boys' bathroom."

Epilogue

Five Influences in My Life—A Media Project by: Ana Wright (Version 2.0)

Dear Mr. Nicholson,

I know we were supposed to write a big report to include with our project, so thank you for the chance to give you this for extra credit. You see, I felt terrible I had to miss out on our project night because I had this totally awesome project prepared. It's a documentary, and I followed people around with a real video camera. I spent hours editing the footage, so you could learn all about them and also all about me. I even got help from my grandpa's girlfriend, Sugar, who it turns out is an amazing filmmaker and my soon-to-be grandmother. (But that's a story for another day!) Anyway. In a dramatic turn of events (those are important in documentaries too), I couldn't actually do the presentation. I know how serious you take your deadlines, so I wanted to show you that I'm serious too. I mean, *yes* it's sort of late. But it's also TWO projects in one! The second half of my project is not a documentary, and there's no fancy musical introduction, but I think you'll be able to learn a lot about who and what influences me this way too.

So along with my documentary, please accept this cast. *Technically*, it's still on my arm, but I've taken good photos of it from all sorts of angles so you can see every single signature and message. When my six weeks are up, I'll make sure you get the real deal. I hope this means you won't dock me points!

As you'll see by what they've written, each of my friends is *so* different. Some of them are supersmart, and some are shy basket cases. Some skip school (but know better), and one's even a giant princess who happens to love sharks. But despite how different they are, they are all great friends to me.

Actually, maybe they're great friends to me *because* of how different they are. I need all of them because they bring out different parts of myself too. And I may not be the best at being great friends back to them yet, but I am trying. All you can do is your best, right? The strong survive, and I know that these friendships will too. Even if it takes a little work sometimes.

Real friends are worth it.

Thanks,
Ana Wright :)
PS
Oh, and in case you're wondering who drew the comic of the giant lizard destroying the school, it was Daz. Feel free to ignore that.

MS. JANE WRIGHT'S PINEAPPLE COOKIES (TOP SECRET!)

Okay, so these are pretty much the only things Mom can make without making the whole kitchen smell like burning—trust me, they are amazing! I've seen Dad eat entire batches of them in an hour!

WHAT YOU'LL NEED:

- 6 tablespoons of room temperature butter
- 6 tablespoons of applesauce
- 1 cup of sugar (plus extra for sprinkling!)
- 2 eggs
- 1 1/4 cups of canned pineapple (don't drain it!)
- 3 cups of flour (regular white flour or whole wheat)
- 1 teaspoon of salt
- 1/2 teaspoon of baking soda
- 1 teaspoon of cinnamon (plus extra for sprinkling!)
- 1/2 teaspoon of nutmeg

WHAT TO DO:

1. Start by preheating your oven to 375°F. Line a baking sheet with parchment paper. (Remember, parchment paper is *not* the same as wax paper! You don't want to smoke up the kitchen!)

2. Mix up the butter, applesauce, sugar, and eggs in a big bowl. Add in your pineapple now. You can use a hand mixer, or you can do it by hand.

3. In a separate bowl, mix up the flour, salt, baking soda, and spices.

4. Mix the wet stuff with the dry ingredients, and make sure it's well combined. It will look sort of gloopy and sticky, but that's okay.

5. Use two spoons to make golf ball–sized cookie balls on your baking sheet. They will spread and puff up in the oven, so leave about 2 inches between them.

6. Sprinkle a little (or a lot!) of leftover cinnamon and sugar over the top of the cookies.

7. Bake them for 10–15 minutes. They will be light brown on the bottom when they're ready.

8. You know the rest—eat them up! Mom always tells me to wait and let them cool before I eat them, but who are we kidding here? Warm cookies are the *best*.

Acknowledgments

I am one lucky writer to have so many amazing people to thank! As always, Kathleen Rushall, you deserve a mountain of gratitude. You're the best agent a writer could ask for and an incredible friend. I love making books with you!

To Aubrey Poole, my brilliant editor! And to superstars Kathryn Lynch, Katherine Prosswimmer, Elizabeth Boyer, Elissa Erwin, Sandra Ogle, Alex Yeadon, and the rest of the wonderful team at Sourcebooks. You have all taught me so much, and I feel lucky every day to work with you. And thank you to Fernanda Viveiros, for working so hard to get Ana's adventures out in the world!

To the kidlit community, the Nerdy Book Club (hey, Nerdcampers!), and my ridiculously wonderful friends! And a shout-out to all of the teachers and educators, working so tirelessly and passionately to promote literacy and find the perfect book for every reader. You are all heroes to me and we owe you the world!

To my parents and family for all the love and support. To Justin, for putting up with revision-brain and providing endless hugs, pizza, and laughs as needed.

And of course, to my awesome readers! When writing a book about friendship, it's hard not to reflect on how lucky you are to have your own set of friends. Thank you all for being such great friends to this series, and for including Ana in your reading lives. Your emails, tweets, and messages make me smile every day! Happy reading!

See how it all began in

HOW TO OUTRUN A CROCODILE WHEN YOUR SHOES ARE UNTIED

By Jess Keating

"Male peacocks use their huge, ornamented tail to attract female attention. Flashy male displays are a common way to successfully obtain a mate."

—*Animal Wisdom*

Mondays are a lot like lions hiding in the tall grass. They are always ready to pounce. And if you're going to school *without* your best friend, Mondays can be just as dangerous. Ever since Liv moved away, I felt like I was walking around with a giant target on my back. I had to pretend like nothing had changed.

But everything had changed.

I kept my head down as I walked to my locker before the bell rang. The halls of our school were buzzing with activity. Summer was almost here, and you could tell it was starting to get to everyone. Even the teachers would stare out the window, like they were looking at a giant slice of pie they wanted to scarf down.

Posters for the end-of-school dance (which they called the "School End Dance"—geniuses) were suspended from the ceilings and people were getting extra touchy-feely all over each other. What is it about upcoming dances and skirt weather that makes girls all eye-batty and guys more rowdy than usual? I mean, it's even on a Monday. Who has a dance on a *Monday*?

Middle school, that's who.

I shoved my backpack into my locker and dug around for a binder. Our final tests were coming up, and my May calendar stared me in the face on my locker door, with each test day marked with a sticker. My math test was the worst of all, looming on my calendar like a giant black hole instead of the cute little unicorn sticker Liv had given me. What if I didn't even pass? I could be stuck in the bottom end of junior high forever. All of the buildup made little flutters of anxiety buzz around in my stomach.

A palm tree sticker on my calendar reminded me about my English assignment. Mrs. Roca has this tradition where she makes us each stand up in front of the room and ramble on for exactly two minutes about a topic that she pulls from a hat. Seriously, she even has this moldy-looking top hat specifically for these little torture sessions. We aren't allowed to say "um" or we lose points. My topic is Harry Houdini, and after coming up with a zillion excuses for the past month on why I wasn't ready, my big day was coming this week.

The only magical guy named Harry that I know anything about had a lightning bolt scar on his forehead, so there is no way I've got two minutes' worth. But mostly, the thought of standing at the front of the room while everybody secretly hopes for me to throw up like I did in fifth grade during group debates was almost enough to make me, well... throw up again. All those eyes just...staring at me.

"Um, can I get into here...?" A low voice interrupted my locker scan. A familiar knocking began in my chest. It was Zack. *The* Zack.

CREATURE FILE

SPECIES NAME: Zackardia Perfecticus

KINGDOM: Junior High

PHYLUM: Tennis Gods; Dimpled Carnivora (LOOK AT HIS DIMPLES!)—targeted crush of Sneerer Clan Apex: Ashley

WEIGHT: Just. Right.

NATURAL HABITAT: Unclear; species has never been seen outside of school habitat. Always has tennis ball in hand, so can probably be found at tennis courts.

FEEDS ON: Sports, video games, and Thursday ravioli at the caf.

LIFE SPAN: Not long enough.

HANDLING TECHNIQUE: I wish.

NOTE ZACKARDIA PERFECTICUS IS KNOWN TO APPEAR OUT OF NOWHERE. ENSURE PROPER HYGIENE AND HAIR CARE TO MINIMIZE EMBARRASSMENT FROM RANDOM ENCOUNTERS. ALSO, LIP GLOSS.

"Hey!" I cleared my throat. Did I just yell that? "Hey, Zack. Nice weather we're having, hmm?"

I actually said that. I wanted to tear out my vocal chords with a pen. I stepped aside so he could get into his locker, which was serendipitously placed beside mine.

I couldn't decide whether it was good or bad luck yet.

Given the last thirty seconds, bad.

Zack was the type of guy that should come with a warning label: Do not look at if you are operating heavy machinery, walking, or trying not to make a complete fool of yourself. Once, Liv caught me doodling a cartoon of Zack looking up at me on a balcony, Romeo and Juliet style. I even drew him holding flowers. *That's* how pathetically sad and insane it makes me having Zack pop up at a moment's notice.

Not only was he seriously the cutest guy in school, Zack was also a tennis star. Girls who couldn't even *spell* tennis showed up to his games. He also had the ability to make me stutter, a development I've noticed since the summer sun had given his hair a decidedly beachy look.

Mmm.

He slid a textbook into his locker with a thud, jerking me from my little daydream. Apparently if Zack is around, I have the attention span of a gnat. I stood there gaping at him, digging around in my head for the perfect, witty thing to say.

"Uh…" was all I came up with.

That's when I heard a high-pitched voice coming from down the hall. I wished for the hundredth time that I was invisible as I peeked past Zack.

The Sneerers.

Three girls swayed their hips as they walked in

their usual line formation. They each had on black skirts with a loose tank top clinging at their hips, each in a different color. I don't know how they managed it, but they always seemed to walk like there was a soundtrack playing for them—only they were the only ones who could hear it.

"Hey, Zack." Ashley gave a flirty wave as she approached us. I ducked my head behind my locker door, hoping they wouldn't notice me.

Ashley, Brooke, and Rayna were the worst part of my day. Every day. You know how some girls you're friends with earlier in school, say, first grade, but then something happens and they start hating on you for no reason?

Yeah. Ashley is nothing like that. We've never been friends. She's always hated me, and she *loves* to feel like she's super mature. She even wears a matching set of earrings and a necklace, which (as she told us a bazillion times) her mother got her when she got her first bra. Because of this (the attitude, the pearl earrings, and the solid B cup), I've always avoided her like a school-borne plague. Tweedledee and Tweedledum stick with her like those little scavenger fish around a shark, eager to get a bite of popularity from her. Actually, Ashley would make a pretty good shark because she's even on the swim team with Rayna. I can't imagine anyone that would *voluntarily* put on a Speedo under those nasty lights, but they seem to have some sort of supergene that makes their blond hair not turn green with all that chlorine. Brooke moved here a year or so ago, so she's currently the lowest rank on Team Sneerer.

CREATURE FILE

SPECIES NAME: Ashleydae Reignus

KINGDOM: Junior High

PHYLUM: Carnivora; Swim Team Goddesses

WEIGHT: I don't know, but they get full after two bites of sushi.

NATURAL HABITAT: The mall, but only the parts that are backlit with pink lighting.

FEEDS ON: The souls and pain of the weak, waterproof mascara, organic food, and *Teen Vogue*; also, my misfortune.

LIFE SPAN: Most witches and monsters in fairytales seek immortality, so...

HANDLING TECHNIQUE: AVOID AT ALL COSTS.

NOTE SPECIES RAYNAA PONTIFICUS AND BROOKENZI SNEEROFIDUS HAVE BEEN FOUND TO BE GENETIC CLONES OF SPECIES NOTED ABOVE.

"Hey, Scales." Ashley's voice dripped with sweetness. You could tell she was aware that Zack was listening by the way her eyes flitted to him every four seconds—such a shark. She swept a lock of blond hair from her eyes. The silver on her earrings twinkled in the light. "I hope there aren't any bugs in your pants today. Must be hard without Liv around to do your hair for you, huh?" She twirled her hair around her fingertip and eyed my ponytail with fake sympathy.

Seriously, ever since my idiot brother let slip that I was named after a snake—an anaconda to be precise—I hadn't heard the end of it. And the whole bug thing—so I accidentally left the house with a pocket full of crickets after feeding some of Daz's snakes. One time. Four years ago. If it hadn't been so mortifying, it would have been funny; they started chirping during Mr. Dixon's grammar lecture, and it sounded exactly like a movie where everybody gets bored. Usually the Sneerers had to face Liv whenever they made fun of me, but now? I am basically target practice.

"Hey, Ashley, did you know that some perfumes are made with whale vomit? Maybe you want to go a little easy on the spritzing tomorrow?"

I *so* wish I'd said that, but the voice belonged to someone else.

I swiveled around wide-eyed to see who had the guts to talk back to Ashley. A tall girl in red warm-up pants was half jogging toward us.

Rebecca!

I gulped and kept my eyes forward, not wanting to make eye contact. Rebecca was Ashley's older sister, and being in eighth grade, she was even more popular (and therefore scarier) than anyone our age in seventh. But she did it without being a kraken. Although it was sort of cool to see someone take a dig at Ashley. How could a nice girl like Rebecca be sisters with Ashley?

"Why don't you shut up, Becca?" Ashley spat at her sister.

Rebecca ignored her and smirked at me. My cheeks burned at the attention. "Ignore her. She's just miffed I beat her time at practice this morning, *again*. Aren't you, *kiddo*?" Rebecca reached out and punched Ashley playfully on the arm before sauntering away to her friends.

See? Some people seem to ooze confidence all over the place. Whereas the only thing I oozed was a bit of prickly sweat under my arms when I was nervous. Which was almost all the time.

I bit my tongue, unable to hide my smile. I guess sometimes the best way to deal with mean ones was to be mean right back? Of course, the thought of saying anything like that to Ashley made me want to lose my breakfast.

Ashley's perfectly stained lips pressed thin, and her face shifted to a grim mask of anger. She makes that face a lot, and it always makes me think her skin is going to melt off and reveal a metal robot skull and a flickering, short-circuited eyeball. I could see it.

She glared at me. "Whatever, geek. Smile all you want, but we'll see how happy you are in English class," she said, puffing up her chest. "I just talked to Mrs. Roca, and she said I could switch my talk with yours. So you'll be talking today, instead of the end of the week," she cooed. "She mentioned something about you putting it off long enough? *You're welcome.*" Ashley's eyes were wide with phony innocence.

My stomach plummeted to the floor. I swear, the devil must take lessons from Ashley. Now what was I going to do?! Two minutes, two minutes... how could I avoid stage fright puking with such short notice?!

About the Author

Jess Keating was nine years old when she brought home a fox skeleton she found in the woods and declared herself Jane Goodall, and not much has changed since then. Her first job was at a wildlife rehabilitation center, where she spent her days chasing raccoons, feeding raptors (the birds, not the dinosaurs!), and trying unsuccessfully to avoid getting sprayed by skunks. Her love of animals carried her through university, where she studied zoology and received a master's degree in animal science, before realizing her lifelong dream of writing a book for kids about a hilarious girl who lives in a zoo.

She has always been passionate about three things: writing, animals, and education. Today, she's lucky enough to mix together all three. When she's not writing books for adventurous and funny kids, she's hiking the trails near her Ontario home, watching documentaries, and talking about weird animal facts* to anyone who will listen. You can email her at jesskeatingbooks@gmail.com, or visit her online at www.jesskeating.com.

*Did you know that grizzly bears can smell food from eighteen miles away?

CREATURE FILE:
Jess Keating

SPECIES NAME: Authorificus Biophiliac

KINGDOM: Ontario, Canada!

PHYLUM: Writers who have a strange love of quirky critters and brave characters; animal nut with a pen

WEIGHT: You dare ask a lady her weight?! Why, I never! Wait, is this before or after I ate that banana split?

NATURAL HABITAT: Outside exploring with a messy notebook, or snuggled up watching nature documentaries with her husband.

FEEDS ON: Grilled apple and cheese sandwiches, popcorn, and pizza.

LIFESPAN: I was born on a sunny summer day in... wait, nobody has time for my life story here. Get it together, Jess.

HANDLING TECHNIQUE: Gets restless inside, so daily walks are essential. Also have significant quantities of caramel corn and extra books on hand in case of emergency.